JACOB'S WAKE

Michael Cook

published with assistance from the Canada Council

Talonbooks
201 1019 East Cordova
Vancouver
British Columbia V6A 1M8
Canada

This book was typeset by Linda Gilbert of B.C. Monthly
Typesetting Service and designed by David Robinson for
Talonbooks.

First printing: December 1975

Talonplays are edited by Peter Hay.

Rights to produce *Jacob's Wake*, in whole or in part, in any
medium by any group, amateur or professional, are retained by
the author and interested persons are requested to apply to his
agent, Renee Paris, 202 1019 East Cordova, Vancouver, British
Columbia V6A 1M8 (604) 254-7558, who is authorized to
negotiate.

ISBN 0-88922-097-2

Jacob's Wake was first performed at Festival Lennoxville in Lennoxville, P.Q., on July 11, 1975, with the following cast:

Mary	Rita Howell
Rosie	Candy Kane
Skipper	Griffith Brewer
Brad	R.H. Thomson
Alonzo	David Calderisi
Winston	Roland Hewgill
Wayne	August Schellenberg

Directed by William Davis
Set and Costume Design by Michael Eagan
Lighting Design by Douglas Buchanan
Sound Design by William Skolnik

Act One

The play can be staged in a variety of ways. The most obvious representation is one of total realism corresponding to the two levels of a typical Newfoundland outport house. The downstairs area is divided into two areas, although the room itself is one kitchen. The centrepiece is a large wood and oil stove, which must be totally functional. To the left is the eating area . . . A simple wooden table, with corresponding chairs, will suffice or a rather hideous chrome set. The sink is on the left wall. Water is piped in from a well during the summer. During the time of the play, however, it can be assumed that the ground is still frozen and that water is being brought in ten gallon plastic buckets. One or two full may be seen between the sink and the stove. There is a window behind the sink.

The area centre and left contains a rocking chair by the fire and, at extreme left, beneath the second, matching window, a rather lumpy day bed stretches against the wall. Cupboards line the wall between the sink and the stove. One of these may be open to display various items of kitchen ware. There would be, on the walls, an oval picture of the

*SKIPPER and his wife, in the heyday of their
youth. One of those incredibly stiff, formal pictures
in which the woman, often a sad faced and beautiful
wooden doll, is dominated by the glaring light
eyes and the walrus moustache of the male. An
illuminated prayer with a sorrowing Christ would
confirm the family's Catholic origins, and perhaps
a sepia tinted photograph of an old iron ship
wallowing in a dead sea. The walls are papered,
and should have that bulky consistency that comes
from placing layer upon layer over the years upon
wooden walls. At backstage centre is the one
entrance, leading to the stairs and exterior. We
should be aware of a small corridor leading offstage
left and the stairs rising, fairly steeply, backstage
centre. The dimensions should be contained so that
at no time is it possible for anyone on stage not to
be aware of, or have to move a great distance to,
anybody else. There should be a sense of confining,
of a claustrophobic intensity which washes against,
and adds to, the emotional tensions built up during
the play.*

*Upstairs, a landing runs centre, with two bedrooms
right and left respectively. The rooms are small,
low-ceilinged, with barely any room for physical
movement other than walking around the beds,
getting into them, or getting objects from the wall.
In the SKIPPER's bedroom, right, there is a narrow
pine highboy or chest of drawers. On it, lies the
SKIPPER's log book and on the wall behind, a
barometer. Beneath the bed is a large chamber pot.*

*Both beds are old-fashioned, metal-framed. Each
room contains a small window, backstage. The
boys' room contains one chair, used for clothes;
the SKIPPER's room, one chair, used by visitors.
Both beds are slightly raked and face the audience.*

*There are obvious small variations on the theme,
but if staged for realistic presentation, then they
must conform to our expectancy. It is in fact,*

minute attention to realistic detail that heightens the progression towards symbolism and abstraction in the action of the play.

An acceptable alternative would be a stark, skeletonized set. The levels would have to remain essentially the same, but a structure as white as bone, stripped of formality, the house equivalent of a stranded hulk of a schooner, only the ribs poking towards an empty sky would serve the play's purpose, and free the director for an existential interpretation of the play.

The stage is in semi-darkness. Sound of storm. A dawn light filters through the windows.

Scene One

ROSIE is sitting in the rocking chair, sewing a patchwork quilt. MARY is at the kitchen table left, marking papers. There is no sound for a long minute, save the slight squeaking of the rocker as ROSIE sews, rocks, sews, rocks. MARY puts down a book and sighs wearily. She stands up, pushing a lock of hair from her eyes, looks at ROSIE, waiting for some comment. None is forthcoming. ROSIE rocks and sews. MARY goes to the stove and checks to see if the kettle is boiling. It is. She crosses to the cupboards left and takes a cup. She rummages again and comes up with a teabag. She crosses to the fridge, pauses and sighs. She turns and puts the cup on the table. She turns back to the refrigerator, opens it and takes out a small bottle of lemon juice. Leaving the door open, she moves to pour a drop of lemon juice into the cup. She moves back and replaces the lemon, and shuts the door. She turns back to the table and sits. She picks up another book, then puts it down. ROSIE sews and rocks.

MARY:
> I just can't do anymore.

ROSIE:
> What, dear.

MARY:
> I said . . . I can't do any more of this marking. It's like washing the same dirty dishes over and over again . . . Without any results.

> *She sips delicately at her tea.*

ROSIE: *resting her quilt in her lap*
> Ye works hard at the teaching, maid. I knows. I wor talking to Sally Ivany t'other day. She boards dat new teacher, Mr. Farrell.

MARY:
> That one! She'd better watch herself then. The man has no principles. I don't understand how people like that ever get into the profession.

ROSIE:
> He got a powerful lot of degrees, Sally said. He's right clever. But he don't play uppity wi' her, she says. He's jest like one of the family. Eats his bit of fish and brewis. Jest loves a salt pork dinner. Sits down an 'as a beer afore dinner wid Rob when 'e's 'ome from the fishing. Right fond of him, she is.

MARY:
> I can imagine! Degrees don't necessarily make good teachers, Rose. Experience is the only teacher. Experience, common sense and a few good old fashioned virtues. There are too many Farrell's about these days, walking into the best jobs, carrying on with their students . . .

ROSIE:
> I said 'as 'ow ye was always at it an' Sally wor surprised. She said he don't ever bring no work 'ome.

10

MARY: *angrily*
Because he doesn't set any homework, that's why. I don't know what things are coming to. They all seem intent upon producing a generation of illiterates and I'm afraid the few of us who are left can hardly stem the tide.

> *A gust of wind shakes the house. There is a moan from SKIPPER upstairs. ROSIE looks up anxiously.*

ROSIE;
Skipper's not sleeping well dese days.

MARY:
Has he ever?

> *She sips her tea.*

I don't suppose I could either, with so much blood on my hands . . . Some of it my own too. Ink, I suppose, has its advantages.

> *There is another gust of wind, and again, SKIPPER moans.*

ROSIE:
I should go up to'n.

> *She makes no move. MARY finishes her tea, gathers up her books and crosses towards the day bed. She bends down and pulls out a wooden chest from beneath it.*

MARY:
Rose, I know you do your best, but don't you think father should be in a place where he can be properly looked after?

ROSE:
In the hospital. In St. John's, ye mean?

MARY:
Something like that. Yes.

She bends again and begins to stack the books into the chest. She lowers the lid and pushes it back underneath.

ROSE:
No, maid. I'd never sleep a wink worrying about'n getting his drop o' rum, knowing 'e'd have no one to tend to'n or read from his book. Having no real voices to talk to.

She rocks and is reflective.

Me own fader now, he were different. When his turn come to be took, he sent me mudder out. To spare 'er, he said. Then he begun to say the psalms. I wor young den. I minds me mother sent me in to look at'n. She reckoned he'd tolerate me where the sight of her would only irritate'n. It wor funny really. Me own fader. Shrivelled face, all yellow it were, an a black hole for a mout' . . . He had nar tooth left in his head . . . The words dribbling out. And . . . Him wi' that old cap on his head like 'e always wore when 'e read the Book to us. I wanted to laugh, but was too afeard.

MARY:
Laugh? And your Father dying?

ROSE:
Ah, but he wor allus gone, maid, working at one t'ing or anudder. I nivir knew'n see. He wor jest somebody dying and I wor just a slip of a maid. Strange. I s'pose dat's why I likes to look after yer fader now. It's like he does for the both of 'n.

A gust of wind. Another moan from SKIPPER. From inside the house, a clock strikes the half hour. MARY finishes stacking her books.

MARY:
There is a difference, Rose. I don't believe father looked
at the Bible once in his life unless it was to mumble a
few words over the men he lost at the ice. And only
then because the law required it.

ROSIE:
Ah well. I must go up to'n.

*She puts her work down in the basket at her side,
heaves herself up out of the chair and crosses to
exit.*

MARY: *exasperated*
For goodness sake, Rose. Leave him be. He's worse than
a child.

ROSIE:
Yes, maid. I 'lows that 'e is. But den, I nivir could say
no to none o' dem neither.

*She goes out. Upstairs, SKIPPER mumbles some-
thing indistinct. MARY looks up. An expression of
near hatred crossing her face.*

MARY:
Why don't you just die and leave us alone.

*A beam of light spills into SKIPPER's room as
ROSIE puts the hall light on. He is sitting upright
in bed, crying soundlessly. ROSIE bustles in, lays
him back, smoothes his forehead, then sits, holding
his hand. A door bangs, loudly, off.*

Winston! Back already.

*She makes for the door to get out before WINSTON
arrives, but just as she reaches it, it is flung open
and BRAD stands there carrying a suitcase. He has
left his topcoat in the outer hall and is wearing a
neat grey suit, surmounted with a clerical collar.*

Despite the traditional mode of his appearance,
there is something wild about his eyes. His hair is
dishevelled.

MARY:

Brad. Thank goodness it's only you.

BRAD:

Hello, Aunt.

He pushes unceremoniously past her, dropping his
suitcase down by the wall.

Where's Mother?

MARY:

Upstairs tending to your Grandfather.

BRAD moves out into the hallway.

BRAD:

Mother! Mother!

MARY:

She's busy. Do you have to announce your arrival?

BRAD:

Yes. Yes, as a matter of fact, I do.

He comes back in.

MARY:

Why? She knows you're coming. God knows, we all do.
You always come on Maundy Thursday though why I've
yet to find out. It's a time when most pastors choose to
stay with their flock, isn't it? But then you always did
make up your own rules.

BRAD:

Not any more, Aunt.

MARY:

What do you mean?

BRAD:
> I . . . Have been replaced. Thrown out.

> *MARY sits as the implications of his words sink in.
> With purposeful energy, as if laying some claim to
> the house, asserting his presence, he begins to make
> himself a cup of tea.*

> My Ministry is ended . . . For the moment. But God's
> work doesn't end when one servant fails. Does it? Does
> it, Aunt Mary?

MARY:
> What have you done now?

BRAD:
> I challenged corruption. That is what I did, single
> handed. But what is one man against the Devil? One
> man against the armies of Cain? I wasn't strong enough,
> Aunt Mary.

MARY:
> Still the same old delusions. Why are you wearing that
> collar?

BRAD:
> The collar?

> *He wrestles with it, takes it off and holds it out.*

> The collar is a symbol. A link in the chain of pride. It
> chokes the soul.

> *He throws the collar to the ground.*

> I am done with false images.

MARY:
> What are you going to do now?

15

> *She is confused, almost defeated. BRAD is an
> unbearable complication in an already intolerable
> situation.*

BRAD:
> Stay here, of course. Wait to be called. Learn to be
> strong again.

MARY:
> No. No, Brad. You can't stay here.

BRAD:
> Why not? This is my house.

MARY:
> And so it is mine. I . . . Your mother and I . . . We can't
> stand any more disruption, Brad. You know what it's
> like here.

> > *BRAD meets her challenge without flinching. She
> > turns from him in disgust.*

> You were always an emotional cripple. Of course you
> failed, as you put it. What made you think you could use
> God as a crutch for your fantasies?

> > *There is still no response from BRAD.*

> Don't you think, at least, that your mother has enough
> to contend with? Or are you going to be content to just
> sit and add your weight to the rest pulling her down to
> an early grave?

BRAD:
> He was despised and rejected of men.

MARY:
> How dare you compare yourself to the Lord. You're
> sick, Brad. Sick. You need help.

> > *With a sudden movement, he takes her hands.*

16

BRAD:
>You're right, Aunt Mary. I do need help. Will you help me? Show me my faults?

MARY: *shaking him off*
>We don't need you here, Brad. Will you get that into your thick head. Go. Go anywhere but here. There's a world out there waiting to be saved.

BRAD:
>But this is where I come from. This is where my work must be.

>>*A door bangs off. ALONZO and WINSTON offstage stamp their boots, wheeze and laugh.*

MARY:
>I think I hear your work coming now.

>>*ALONZO and WINSTON appear in the doorway. Arms round each other, singing, palpably the worse for wear. Like a travesty of an old music hall duo, they try to get through the door together and get stuck.*

ALONZO and
WINSTON:
>In Dublin's city where I did dwell
>Lived a butcher's boy I loved right well.
>He courted me . . .

>>*The crescendo is broken as ALONZO staggers through the door first, nearly falling.*

ALONZO:
>Christ, Father. You're getting as fat as a pig.

>>*He spots BRAD and peers at him. WINSTON follows him in.*

>Well, well, well. It's the Reverend Blackburn. How are ye, Brad?

17

He slaps him on the back and nearly knocks both BRAD and himself over. He clutches him for support. WINSTON crosses to the day bed as MARY rises and crosses to the door to escape.

WINSTON:
'Tis the Prodigal himself, come fer to wish us a Happy Easter. A Happy Easter, son.

He belches loudly.

MARY:
It's Maundy Thursday. A few minutes from now it will be Good Friday.

WINSTON:
Oh. 'Tis mauzy Thursday, is it? I t'ought the weather were a bit queer.

ALONZO finds this very funny. MARY surveys the scene grimly and points to BRAD.

MARY:
For once, Winston, your besotted brain has stumbled upon a truth. You should welcome Brad with open arms. That is, if you can open them. Your second mistake has come home. To roost.

She exits. WINSTON sits up, puzzled.

WINSTON:
What did she say?

ALONZO:
Dunno, boy. Something about a dicky bird.

BRAD: *crossing to his father and holding out his hand*
Hello, father. I trust you're well.

WINSTON catches his hand and pulls him down on the day bed.

18

WINSTON:
I think I wor, until I saw ye. Lonz. Lonz, b'y. D'ye hear that. He trusts I'm well.

ALONZO:
That's what all them religious say when yer dying.

WINSTON:
That's right too.

ROSIE enters and goes straight to the stove to fill a jug of hot water from the kettle.

ROSIE:
Oh my. Yer all back. I jest bin sitting up wid yer fader, Winston. He's bin right upset tonight.

BRAD, disengaging himself from WINSTON, crosses to ROSIE.

BRAD:
Mother . . .

He puts out his arms for an embrace. She turns towards him, holding the kettle.

ROSIE:
Why, Brad. I t'ought I heard ye when I wor upstairs . . . How are ye? . . .

BRAD:
Mother . . . I've come home.

ROSIE crosses to the kitchen area. BRAD follows her.

ROSIE:
I knows, son. Ye allus comes to see us Easter. Yer a good boy.

BRAD:
>No, mother. You don't understand. You see, I've come home for good. I've . . . Left the church.

WINSTON:
>That's what Mary meant! Well be the Lard Jesus, what have I done to deserve that?

ALONZO:
>I dunno, father. It might do us all good to have the family conscience restored to the fold.

WINSTON:
>Family pain in the arse. That's what he is. Always wor, now I comes to think of it.

BRAD: *trying to maintain a semblance of dignity*
>Father . . . I've had a difficult day . . .

>>*ALONZO has found the collar on the floor and gleefully tries it on.*

WINSTON:
>So have I, son, and ye've made it worse . . .

BRAD:
>I don't expect you to understand . . . I don't expect anyone to share my burdens . . . But a little welcome . . .

ALONZO: *prancing about the kitchen, the collar firmly fastened* How do I look, mother?

>>*ROSIE is pouring herself a cup of tea. She turns and laughs, the laughter of shocked delight.*

ROSIE:
>Yer some shocking boy. Have ye no respect? Take it off.

ALONZO: *in a dreadful imitation of Garner Ted Armstrong* I'll take your bets now . . . You're all gamblers . . . We all gamble with our souls . . . Yes, our souls . . . So I'll

take your bets now on the second coming. What's that,
sir . . . You haven't had one since you were eighteen . . .

ROSIE: *putting down her tea and chasing ALONZO round the
room, laughing* Lonz. Lonz! Now you give me dat.

> *He dodges round her. She pauses breathless and
> laughing at the table.*
>
> *WINSTON staggers to the fridge and gets a beer.
> He raises it and drains half the bottle in one gulp.
> Sighing with satisfaction, he wipes his face with the
> back of his hand. He belches loudly and begins to
> sing.*

WINSTON:
> Here's a health to ye, Father O'Flynn
> Drink it in ginger or drink it in gin . . .

BRAD: *anguished*
Mother.

ALONZO: *sternly to WINSTON*
Today's sermon will, yet again, be on the evils of drink.
Last week . . . Last week, the collection amounted to
two dollars thirteen cents and one Japanese yen. And
yet only the previous night many of you . . . Yes,
women too . . . Spent triple, nay, quadruple, in fact,
a hell of a lot more than that at that palace of sin . . .
The Blue Flamingo . . .

> *WINSTON collapses on a kitchen chair. ROSIE too
> laughs.*

BRAD:
Mother. Stop them.

ROSIE:
Oh, don't mind them, b'y. Dey's only having a bit of
fun wid ye. Now come on and I'll git ye a lunch. Ye
must be starved come all dat way.

> *He stands uncertain. ALONZO capers round him.*

ALONZO:
>
> Brad, Brad, wouldn't
> Listen to his Dad,
> Went to be a preacher
> Cos his folks they was all bad

Whooooo . . . eeeee

ROSIE:
> And so ye are whooping and hollerin' and carryin' on.
> Set the table, the lot of ye. I'll get ye a cup o' tay.

WINSTON:
> Who needs tea? Rosie, get Brad a beer.

BRAD:
> No thank you, father.

WINSTON:
> But ye've left the ministry. Ye said so.

BRAD:
> Yes. I have but . . .

WINSTON:
> Then ye've no call not to be normal like the rest of us.
> Lonz, git a beer into him.

> *WINSTON hands ALONZO his beer. ALONZO*
> *stalks BRAD. ROSIE watches half shocked, half*
> *laughing.*

ALONZO:
> Come on, Brad. Here, boy. Here. Ye've dropped yer
> collar now. It's jest like the ould days.

BRAD:
> I can't, Alonzo. It's not like that.

WINSTON:
What is it like then, son? Ye comes home and tells us
yer back wit' the family, so ye must takes what ye gets.
Like the rest of us.

*ALONZO has forced BRAD back onto the day bed.
ROSIE is laughing outright. ALONZO forces the
bottle to BRAD's mouth.*

ALONZO:
Come on, baby. Drink . . . Drink . . .

*BRAD wrestles furiously. The beer pours all over
him. WINSTON and ROSIE laugh aloud. BRAD,
almost hysterical, succeeds in pushing ALONZO
back. He falls on all fours. BRAD leaps up frenziedly
wiping his mouth.*

BRAD:
Damn you. Damn you.

He is close to tears.

ROSIE:
Alright, b'ys. 'Tis gone far enough.

WINSTON:
Nice words from a man of the cloth.

ALONZO:
And assault and battery.

*BRAD rushes for the door, but WINSTON, sensing
his move, blocks his way. BRAD moves round the
room like a trapped animal.*

ROSIE: *alarmed*
Dat's enough now, Winston. Stop it.

BRAD: *screaming*
I haven't given up anything. That's a symbol. A collar is
just a symbol . . . I haven't given up on God.

23

WINSTON: *moving back away from the door*
Stay around here long enough and He'll give up on ye.

BRAD:
Never. No. Never. He won't desert me.

> *Unnoticed, WAYNE has appeared in the door. He's immaculately suited and carries an executive over-night case.*

WAYNE:
Well, well. The same old animal farm, I see.

ALONZO:
Welcome home, brother. Ye've missed the sermon, but yer just in time for the collection.

ROSIE: *crossing to welcome him*
Wayne.

> *He kisses her.*

Yer father said ye'd not be coming dis year.

> *She takes his case and puts it behind the day bed. WAYNE comes on in.*

WAYNE:
Well, mother, I have to fight through the paper this high to get into the office, but it can wait another day or so. And I've some constituents with a few problems to see up this way . . . So here I am.

ROSIE:
We're right pleased ye could come, aren't we, Winston?

WINSTON:
I'm overjoyed, maid.

ALONZO:
Who are ye trying to kid, Wayne. Seeing constituents on Good Friday! Ye're not that conscientious. There's something else in the wind. Wouldn't be anything to do with me, would it? A contract or two?

WAYNE:
Who knows.

WINSTON:
Come to see me, didn't ye, son? Unlike a few I could mention, he's proud of his father. Talks about me all the time in that House of Assembly . . . To the Minister o' Welfare.

He chuckles.

WAYNE: *ignoring him*
Where's Aunt Mary?

ROSIE:
Oh, she's gone. Must've gone to bed while I wor upstairs wid yer grandfader. That wor afore Brad come. Poor Brad. They bin tormentin' 'im somethin' terrible.

BRAD has been standing stiffly by the window, trying to bring himself under control. WAYNE crosses to him and holds out his hand.

WAYNE:
Hi, Brad.

BRAD: *turning, ignoring the hand . . . still dripping slightly*
You!

WAYNE:
Good God. Have you been drinking?

WINSTON and ALONZO laugh.

BRAD:
Devil. You sent them. You did, didn't you?

25

WAYNE:
    I don't know what you're talking about.

BRAD:
    Oh yes, you do. Judas!

    He rushes out.

ROSIE:
    Dat's dem two, see. Nivir did take much to a ribbin',
    Brad didn't. I'd better go and see'n settled.

    She makes for the door and turns.

    He'll be sleepin' wid ye, Lonz. Ye don't mind, do ye?

WAYNE:
    Why should he. Lonz has never been particular about
    who he slept with.

ALONZO:
    Watch it, brother. Watch it.

    ROSIE exits.

WINSTON:
    Want a drink, son?

    He proffers a beer.

    Oh yis. I'm sorry, sir.

    He tugs his forelock.

    Beer's a working man's drink, i'n it?

WAYNE: *mocking*
    Jesus, fader. Then what are ye doing drinkin' it.

    *WINSTON goes to the dresser, opens a drawer,
    produces a bottle of moonshine, holds it up to the
    light and eyes it with great satisfaction.*

WINSTON:

> Now . . . That's a good brew. One of the best I ever
> made, though I says it meself.

> *He puts the bottle on the table.*

> Lonz. Get a jug of hot water, boy. Wayne, me son. Git
> the mugs.

> *It's a traditional part of the family ritual. WINSTON
> gets sugar from the dresser and one teaspoon from a
> drawer. WAYNE gets three mugs. ALONZO pours
> hot water from the kettle into a substantial aluminum
> jug. All three deposit their burdens, pause and sit,
> almost simultaneously. The irony is that whereas
> the rules of the ritual have evolved into killing
> games, the unifying structure remains the same.
> WINSTON pours and mixes a drink.*

> Now, boys. Let's celebrate the annual family re-union.

WAYNE:

> What family? What union?

> *WINSTON eyes him steadily. WAYNE, unmoved,
> helps himself to a drink.*

WINSTON:

> Now, b'y. I knows ye've gone up in the world. Weren't
> nowhere else to go from here, was there? But ye still
> comes back every year. Or nearly every year. They must
> be something in it.

ALONZO:

> The thrill of disaster.

WINSTON:

> A good crack.

ALONZO:

> No, b'y. Love. That's what it is. Love.

27

WINSTON:
> I 'lows I nivir t'ought o' that.

> *They both laugh. WAYNE allows himself a grin. He knows the game, the rules, and showing emotion isn't one of them. ROSIE re-enters.*

ROSIE:
> Oh. Ye's all settled den. I bin talking to Brad, Winston. He's some upset. Seems like dey t'rew him out. Now, isn't dat shockin'? After all he done for dem too.

ALONZO:
> About time they come to their senses. I heard stories about him, mother, that ye wouldn't have been so proud of.

WAYNE:
> Me too.

WINSTON:
> Oh. What wor that then? I t'ought he wor incapable of sin.

WAYNE:
> He was becoming a damned nuisance. Moved one community from a decent fishing ground to a hole in the bog. Pestered us and Ottawa for grants of one kind or another. Even tried a little arson though we couldn't prove it.

ALONZO:
> So he was right. Ye got rid of him.

WAYNE:
> Did I say that?

ALONZO:
> Ye didn't have to. I can see I'll have to watch you, boy. Yer getting dangerous.

WAYNE:
> Thanks for the compliment.

WINSTON:
> Jesus. Politics! Let's get off the subject afore I pukes.
> Rosie . . . Rosie, maid. Git the cards, will ye?

> *In the interior, a clock strikes twelve. ROSIE*
> *fetches a pack of cards.*

ROSIE:
> Oh my. 'Tis twelve already.

> *She yawns widely.*

> Shall I go up and git the bed warm, Winston?

WINSTON:
> Ye can do what ye likes, maid. I 'lows it'll take more
> than warmth to dress me leg tonight.

> *During the following speech, ROSIE exits and*
> *re-appears with a handful of splits for lighting*
> *the fire in the morning. She lowers the oven door,*
> *places the wood in the oven and leaves the door*
> *down.*

WAYNE:
> Father. For God's sake.

WINSTON:
> He allus wor squeamish, Lonz. I suppose that's what
> they calls sensitivity.

ALONZO:
> Is it? Jes', fader. Ye're a walking encyclopaedia. I learns
> something every time I comes here.

ROSIE:
> Goodnight then, b'ys.

29

WAYNE:
> Goodnight, mother.

ALONZO:
> 'Night.

> *ROSIE exits. WINSTON picks up the cards.*

WINSTON:
> First Jack deals?

> *They nod. He rapidly spins round the cards off the*
> *top of the pack. The first Jack falls to WAYNE.*

> Jesus, if he fell off a skyscraper, he'd land in a pile o'shit.

> *He throws the pack at WAYNE, who shuffles them*
> *and begins to deal. They are playing one hundred*
> *and twenties. The cards are dealt, five apiece, in*
> *blocks of two and three.*

ALONZO:
> I blames Aunt Mary for Wayne, father. Shoving all
> them books and morals into his head when he were
> young. Unhealthy, I says.

> *All three examine their cards, WAYNE in particular*
> *making sure that no one can catch a glimpse of his*
> *hand.*

WAYNE:
> Jealousy will get you nowhere. Anyway, you haven't
> done too badly out of me, one way or another.

WINSTON:
> Jealous! Of you! I'll go twenty. I wouldn't change me
> peace of mind fer all yer House of Assemblies.

ALONZO:
> Twenty five. I make more money than he does anyway.

WAYNE:
I'll take your twenty five. If you want to live by selling
watered booze and importing prostitutes as strippers
you're welcome to it.

ALONZO:
There's more than one way of prostitution.

WINSTON:
Make it, son.

ALONZO:
And for me.

WAYNE:
Diamonds!

WINSTON:
I nivir told ye, Lonz, about the time we 'ad to get
Wayne circumcised when he wor little. I'll take three.

ALONZO:
No. Ye didn't. Two fer me.

> *WINSTON discards and accepts three cards from
> WAYNE. ALONZO, likewise. WAYNE goes
> through the discards, ignores them and takes two
> cards.*

WINSTON:
'Is mother wor some proud of his bird. It wor about
t'ree inches long when he wor borned.

WAYNE: *rattled*
Your down, father. Your down!

> *WINSTON plays and continues unperturbed.*

WINSTON:
All the neighbours come in to look at'n. It wor the
eighth wonder of the world, boy. Even yer Aunt Mary
were excited, though she didn't know why.

WAYNE:
  For God's sake, Alonzo. Play, will you. Or pack it in.

ALONZO: *plays*
  What happened?

WAYNE: *plays*
  Can't you ever get your mind out of the gutter, father?

WINSTON:
  It wor keeping yer cock out of the gutter that worried
  us. An' the Doctors said if it wor real, ye'd nivir be no
  good to no one, 'cept an old ewe maybe.

  He plays.

ALONZO: *chuckling and beginning to sing*

> Ewe take the high road
> An' I'll take the low road

WAYNE:
  Play!

  ALONZO plays.

  You're just trying to beat this hand. It won't work . . .

  He takes the trick.

WINSTON:
  Anyways, we took 'n to St. John's. Yer mother took a
  photograph of 'n afore we left, just in case they cut'n
  right off.

WAYNE:
  Your card, father. Your card. That's the Jack of Trumps.

WINSTON:
  So it is. Well, I got nar' one.

  He throws away.

ALONZO:
> What happened? The five of trumps, Wayne.

WAYNE: *shouting*
> It can't be. I just played that.

ALONZO:
> You're mistaken, brother. I wondered why you took my twenty five in the first place.

> *WAYNE searches back through his tricks, finds the offending card and throws it in front of ALONZO.*

> You accusing me of cheating.

WINSTON:
> Like all politicians, Lonz. They can't bear to lose, even to family and friends.

WAYNE:
> I say you cheated.

SKIPPER:
> Jacob! Jacob!

WINSTON:
> There he goes. Slippin' out through the Narrows agin.

ALONZO:
> What happened?

WAYNE:
> You cheated.

SKIPPER:
> Jacob . . .

WINSTON:
> It wor all skin. They was nothing there. Nothing at all. Smallest damn thing ye ever did see.

ALONZO collapses in hysterics. WAYNE, furious, strides round the table. Delves into ALONZO's pocket and comes up with a set of trump cards.

WAYNE:
You disgusting, cheating pimp. No more favours, d'you hear. No more contracts. Not from me. Not from anybody in this government.

ALONZO: *unmoved*
Did it ever grow?

WINSTON:
Never, b'y. Never. That's why he'd only let Aunt Mary give'n 'is weekly bath. An' that went right on 'til he wor thirteen or so.

ALONZO shrieks with laughter.

WAYNE: *shouting*
Stop lying. Stop lying, for Christ's sake.

MARY appears in the door, dressed in a voluminous nightgown.

MARY:
What in the name of Christian charity is going on in this house? The noise is enough to wake the dead.

Coming forward, she sees WAYNE.

Wayne.

SKIPPER:
I nivir sent the starm, Jacob. Ye can't blame me for that.

WINSTON:
The dead arose and appeared to many.

WAYNE:
I'm sorry, Aunt.

He attempts to recover composure, moves round the table, putting on his jacket which has been discarded at the beginning of the game. WINSTON watches him carefully, waiting for a further opportunity. ALONZO's chuckles punctuate the brief silence. MARY moves to WAYNE and puts her hand on his arm.

MARY:
> You shouldn't let them do this to you, Wayne.

WINSTON:
> That's right, maid. We shouldn't 'a let 'em do it to'n in the first place, I 'lows.

MARY:
> Do what? What drunken gibberish are you on with now?

WAYNE:
> For the love of . . . Shut up.

> *To MARY.*

> Each time I walk into this house, I lose my sanity. You'd think by now I'd know better.

MARY:
> You shouldn't come.

WINSTON:
> But he do, maid. He do. And we all knows why, eh, Lonz?

ALONZO: *sputtering*
> For his bath.

> *WAYNE goes for ALONZO.*

MARY:
> Wayne. Don't. That's just what they want.

> *WAYNE draws back.*

35

WAYNE:
Don't worry, Aunt.

To WINSTON and ALONZO.

This is definitely the last time, d'you hear? You've
played your last game of cards at my expense, the pair
of you.

*He crosses to the day bed, picks up his case and
walks out into the livingroom with MARY.*

ALONZO:
God, father. That were worth coming home for. Father!

*WINSTON slumps back on the chair, mouth open
and begins to snore. ALONZO shakes his head,
gets up, moves as if to exit, but the old force of
habit pulls him back. He closes the bottle, puts it
back on the chest of drawers. He picks up the
scattered cards and crosses, the cards in his hand,
to the stair door.*

Mother. Mother.

*He goes back to the table and puts the cards in the
box. He puts them away. He tries to lift WINSTON
and gets him as far as centre, then the pair collapse.
ALONZO gets up as ROSIE enters, tieing her
nightdress about her.*

There ye are. Help me to git him upstairs, will ye?

*The two manage to raise WINSTON and begin to
drag him towards the door.*

Jesus. He never used to be this heavy.

ROSIE:
I knows, b'y. 'Tis all the beer, I suppose. What wor all
the racket about?

ALONZO: *laughing*
> Oh nothing, mother. Jest a friendly game of cards. Jest like the old days . . .

> *They exit. The lights dim, except upstairs on SKIPPER. He is listening intently. There is an ominous gust of wind, the beginnings of a storm. He nods and smiles. He folds his hands and lies back. The light fades.*

Scene Two

> *The following morning. A cold dawn light filters through the windows. A savage gust of wind shakes the house, then subsides to a threatening moan. ROSIE bustles in with a kerchief tied about her head. Her first action is to turn on the radio before she lights the fire. As the radio fades in with a hymn, she hums and part sings along with it, putting in the splits, checking the oil burner, lighting the wood, filling kettles, making general preparations for breakfast. On the radio, John Beverley Shea sings.*

> There is a green hill
> Far away beside a city wall
> Where our Dear Lord was crucified
> Who died to save us all.

> *MARY enters.*

ROSIE:
> Good morning, Mary.

MARY:
> Is it? Have you looked outside?

ROSIE:
> What's dat, maid?

MARY:
> I asked, have you looked outside?

ROSIE:
> No, maid. Dis time of year I prefers not to do dat. 'Tis right depressing!

> *MARY crosses to the window. She looks out. She returns to the rocking chair. The hymn continues.*

MARY:
> We're in for a storm it seems. It's snowing hard already. Just the excuse some people will be looking for, I suppose.

ROSIE:
> What for? Nobody's working today, girl.

MARY:
> I know that, dear. I really shouldn't myself. But I have so much to do before term begins.

> *She crosses and reaches under the day bed for the trunk with the exercise books in it.*

ROSIE:
> Oh dat's not work in dat way, Mary. Teaching is the Lard's work, dey say.

MARY: *settling down with some books on the day bed*
> You're a good woman, Rose. Where's Winston? Although I should know better than to ask. Still sleeping it off, I suppose.

ROSIE:
> He'll be down in a minute, maid. Likes to come down to a warm kitchen, Winston do. It sets 'im up fer the day like. And when he's 'appy, we's all happy.

MARY:
> Are we? Winston's happiness spells disaster for those of us who don't enjoy alcohol or obscenity. Do you know what they did to Wayne last night?

ROSIE:
> Dey was only having a bit o' fun wid'n, maid. Dey allus done dat.

MARY:
> Fun is it.

> *She corrects some mistakes and sighs.*

> Rosie. Wouldn't it be nice, just for once, if you could stay in bed one morning and come down to a nice warm kitchen?

ROSIE:
> Stay in bed. Me.

> *She laughs.*

> I'd be lost in dat big bed all be meself, maid.

MARY:
> I've got my doubts about that. But you're probably right. Winston would set fire to the woodbox.

> *The last lines of the last verse of the hymn are heard.*

> Oh dearly, dearly has He loved,
> And we must love Him too,
> And trust in His redeeming blood
> And try His works to do.

> That's a lovely hymn, even if it is Anglican!

ANNOUNCER:
> Good morning, Newfoundland, on this Good Friday morning. The sponsors of our Sacred Music Hour would

like to remind you that at the time of bereavement, their trained, dignified and sympathetic staff will attend to your personal needs with discretion. And now we continue with the stirring hymn, "Stand Up, Stand Up for Jesus" . . .

There is an enraged roar from SKIPPER's bedroom upstairs.

SKIPPER:
Fer Jesus sake, Mary . . . Turn that damn thing off . . .

The light goes up slowly to reveal SKIPPER in bed, struggling to prop himself upon the pillows and at the same time to retrieve his stick, a vicious looking piece of polished oak, from the side of the bed. Having done both things, he begins to thump loudly with the stick on the floor. The singing continues.

MARY: *angrily*
I'll drown him out.

She turns up the radio volume. SKIPPER renews his banging.

SKIPPER:
And where's me rum? I wants me rum.

MARY: *shouting up*
It'll do ye no harm to hear a hymn or two on this one day of the year. And Dr. Burr said you were to have no more spirits!

SKIPPER:
I don't give a tinker's cuss what the doctor said and if that thing isn't turned off this minute, I'll come downstairs and knock its brains out . . .

He accompanies this with terrifying blows of the stick.

MARY: *shouting*

Don't be talking such nonsense. Ye haven't been out of that bed for thirty years and what miracles will occur this day aren't likely to happen in this Godforsaken house.

SKIPPER: *hammering furiously*

Ye bousy ol 'bitch. I'll . . .

ROSIE, alarmed, scuttles to the radio and turns it off.

ROSIE:

Now, Mary, ye knows how he is. And he's not much longer fer dis world, God rest his soul . . .

MARY:

I've got my doubts about that . . .

ROSIE:

What's dat, maid?

MARY:

Whether God will rest his soul.

SKIPPER has been straining to hear this conversation. He leans back on his pillows and laughs, a ravaged, toothless laugh.

SKIPPER:

Heh. She's turned it off anyways. Cantankerous as a starved gannet. Can't believe she ever sprung from these loins. Mustn't have known what I was about then, mother. A poor substitute for Jacob, so she was.

He lolls back and pauses. The lights fade on the kitchen below. There is the sound of a storm building.

A man should be surrounded with ould friends in his dyin'. Ould shipmates. Not a bunch of harpies. All those

brave boys . . . Iced down . . . Rolling in the Labrador
current.

*He sits up suddenly, staring straight ahead and
roars.*

SKIPPER:
Over the side, lads. Over the side. Look lively, now. Gaff
and sculp. Gaff and sculp.

He sits back. The wind howls in his mind.

The ice and the sun and the brave boys.

He sits up roaring.

Git after them, damn ye. East . . . To the East. To hell
wi' the starm. Ye can face into it. They must be East.

The sound of the storm increases in intensity.

De yer worst, ye howling black devil. I'm not afraid o'
ye, nor me boys neither. Out of my way. I'll git the
men. Aye and the swiles too. I defy ye. I defy ye.

*He swings with his stick at the imagined, but real
enemy, the spirit of death, the spirit of the ice.
The storm fades. He stares into the nightmare of
the past then sinks back, exhausted. The lights fade
on him and come up in the kitchen. WINSTON is
warming his hands over the stove. MARY is sitting
on the day bed, surrounded with books. ROSIE is
laying the table.*

MARY:
First you and that insolent bar owner last night. And
now father. He does it deliberately. I'm sure of it. Every
time there's a storm, roaring and blaspheming, damning
us all with his tortured conscience. If I had my way . . .

WINSTON:
Ye'd have him in the Mental, along with the rest o' the family. And have the house to yerself then, eh? Or p'raps ye'd keep Rosie to look after yer ladylike needs. Go on wid ye. Give the old man his rum. It's a holiday.

MARY:
Holiday is it. Everyday's a holiday for some folk. And this the occasion of The Lord's death. I'll remind you, brother, that the origin of holiday is holy day.

WINSTON:
Ye're not at school now, Miss! And I'm not one of yer students, thanks be to God.

MARY:
Amen to that.

WINSTON:
He's had his rum now everyday since the day he wor borned. One drop, more or less, won't affect his chances of salvation.

MARY:
And a day's work, more or less, won't affect yours. But that would be more of a miracle than getting old Lazarus up there to leave his room.

WINSTON: *exaggeratedly clutching his heart . . . on the wrong side* Now, sister. We've been over all that before. That murmur in me heart . . . I can hear it now.

MARY:
If that's all we did hear from you, life might be easier in this house of useless men. I'm no feminist, but I swear to God I know why the movement was started.

WINSTON:
Ye'd hardly qualify as a feminist, would you? Aren't they all women in that?

43

ROSIE:

> Now don't ye two start at it again. Come and sit down, Mary, whiles I gits yer breakfast . . .

MARY:

> I'll be there in a minute.

> *MARY, glaring at WINSTON, crosses into the eating area and sits. ROSIE pours her a cup of tea, then scurries back to the stove where a variety of pots and pans are bubbling away.*

ROSIE:

> It's some nice having all the family home for the holiday. Just like when dey was growing up!

MARY:

> Wayne was down at Christmas.

ROSIE:

> Well, it's different at Christmas. Dere's so much to do. And den dere's all the visiting. Dere's hardly time to see yer own. But dis time, dere's no celebratin' to git in the way. What are ye doin', Winston?

> *WINSTON has crossed to the fridge. He opens it and rummages for a beer.*

WINSTON:

> Getting meself a beer.

ROSIE:

> Before yer bit of bologna?

MARY:

> He's celebrating the family reunion, aren't you, brother?

WINSTON:

> Right, sister. Life is one long celebration.

> *He opens the beer, takes a swig from the bottle and sighs with satisfaction.*

Never ye mind about me, Mary.

He belches loudly and crosses to the day bed.

Ye just get right on with all that marking ye've got to
do. What is it this time?

*He picks up one of the books, beer in one hand,
book in the other.*

MARY: *rising*
Leave those books alone, you savage . . .

WINSTON: *declaiming*
"Daffodils," by William Wordsworth. By Mary Freak for
Miss Blackburn, Grade 6. "Daffodils is a poem all about
yellow flowers called daffodils. The poet is flying in an
aeroplane and looking down through the clouds, he
sees . . ."

*MARY rushes across to WINSTON and tries to
seize the book. They struggle.*

MARY:
Give me that, you illiterate . . . Give me that book . . .

*The book is torn in half. WINSTON collapses on
the day bed, laughing. MARY falls back centre,
clutching the remnants of Mary Freak's book. She
is nearly in tears. ROSIE rushes to comfort her.*

ROSIE:
Winston, ye shouldn't have . . . Whatever will Mary say
to the Principal.

WINSTON: *unrepentant*
Well, what's she doing bringing all that stuff home? Just
does it to make us feel guilty, that's all. Ye can see the
words like little balloons at the back of her head every
time she picks up one of those poor kids' essays . . .

He mimics.

WINSTON:

> Ye're all lazy and ungrateful and I've spent the best years of my life looking after ye and father . . .

> *He goes to the stove, lifts the lid, spits expertly into the flames and replaces it.*

> Hell, if she'd taken the trouble to roll about in the grass a bit when she wor young, it might've made a difference. Some foolish fella might've married'n. Too late now, I allows.

ROSIE:

> Winston! Now dat's enough, boy.

WINSTON:

> Who else would have her now except we?

ROSIE:

> I swear to God ye'd never know Mary wuz your sister! I'm not going to have the day spoilt afore it's even started. Ye had yer bit o' devilment last night wi' Lonz. Now give over, boy.

> *MARY has gone across to the day bed and is collecting the remainder of the assignments. She has recovered her composure and is icy.*

MARY:

> It's alright, Rose. It's all the thanks I can expect from him. He was always destructive of anything he couldn't understand. Even as a small boy. In fact, there was a time when everyone thought he was retarded.

WINSTON: *laughing*

> And ye've nivir changed yer mind, have ye, sister?

> *He fills his pipe. MARY stacks her books away.*

> That's the one thing we have in common though, Mary. Neither one of us 'as changed a bit and we in't about to. Take me now . . . Born retarded . . . Dyin' . . . At least

I thinks that's I'm doing . . . Still retarded. And Mary . . .
Born a virgin. Getting ready to be laid out a virgin . . .
Widout any of the benefits of an Immaculate Conception.

ROSIE:
Winston! Dey's no call fer dat kind of talk.

MARY:
Don't worry about me, Rose. I can look after myself.
It's you I feel sorry for, dear. Plodding along after all
these years with a man who's an expert at two things.
Making moonshine and cheating the Welfare.

WINSTON:
That's right, Mary. Haven't ye heard o' specialization?
'Tis what everyone has to do these days.

ROSIE:
'Tis not as bad as dat, Mary.

She is wistful.

I wishes sometimes ye wouldn't fight so much. But den
the two of ye nivir got on and dat's it, I suppose. An'
I'm luckier dan me mother an dey whose men nivir
spent a minute at home, traipsin' off to the Labrador or
Toronto or such. I allus reckoned it wor his life to do
what he would wit', providin' dey was a bit of food in
the house and wood fer the stove . . .

WINSTON crosses to ROSIE and slaps her backside.

WINSTON:
That's my Rosie. Fat and comfortable and mindin' her
own business. Aye, and warm on a cold night too.

He swings on MARY.

But ye, ye frozen wharf junk. Ye wouldn't know anything
about that part of life now, would ye?

47

MARY crosses to the table and sits down. WINSTON follows her, leans across at her, breathing into her face. She averts it in disgust.

WINSTON:

Turn away ye might. I seed ye once. Through the winder of the school house. Strappin' some poor kid across the hand, and it a bitter morning, until he screamed fer ye to stop.

MARY slaps him across the face. For a moment, it looks as if WINSTON is about to spit in her face in reply, but ROSIE hurriedly intervenes.

ROSIE:

Winston . . .

She pushes him away from the table.

Why don't ye take a drop of rum and sugar up to yer fader?

She hurriedly opens a cupboard, takes down a bottle of rum, pours a glass, shoves the glass into WINSTON's hand and hurries across to the stove, where she fills a jug with hot water.

Ye knows how he likes to talk to ye.

WINSTON:

Doesn't talk to me. Talks to ghosts.

ROSIE:

I know, dear.

She crosses back with the jug and gives it to WINSTON.

But 'tis good company for'n. Go on now.

She tries to shoo him out.

Go on, afore dere's anymore trouble.

WINSTON:
Who's good company, Rosie. Me? Or the ghosts?

He drains the glass of rum, collects the bottle and moves to exit.

Alright, alright. I'm going. And mind, woman, that there's a clean cloth on the table for the children when they finally haul their arses out of bed. We must make some effort to keep up appearances, eh, Mary?

MARY:
We! You could turn Buckingham Palace into a beer parlour.

WINSTON chuckles and exits, moving up on the stairs.

ROSIE:
My, my. Dey's always somet'ing, in't there? I'd better start the fish. The boys'll be down soon.

MARY:
Boys! Rosie, they're all grown men, quite capable of looking after themselves. I'm sure Wayne, at least, wouldn't expect you to put yourself out.

ROSIE:
I knows.

With satisfaction.

But old habits dies 'ard.

In the boy's room, upstairs left, BRAD suddenly sits bolt upright.

BRAD: *shouting*
Fire . . . Fire . . . Mother . . .

WINSTON pauses on the landing outside the room.

ROSIE:
>That's Brad having one of his dreams agin. The doctor said it wor on account of.

BRAD:
>Alonzo. Wake up. Wake up.

ALONZO:
>What . . .

BRAD:
>I had a dream of fire. Everything burning . . .

ALONZO: *leaping out of bed*
>Fire . . . Where? . . .

MARY:
>On account of what?

ROSIE:
>H'imagination. Dat's what 'e said.

BRAD:
>Flames reaching up to the Heavens. And all the souls of the damned crying out. Yes. And you were there Alonzo. And father. Burning.

>*The lights go up in the boys' bedroom as ALONZO, clad in a scanty pair of boxer shorts, releases the blind. BRAD is sitting stiffly up in the bed. He is wearing thick woollen combinations. WINSTON has stayed to listen at the door.*

ALONZO:
>Oh, is that all? I thought it were something serious.

>*ALONZO shivers back to the bed and climbs in.*

>Mother. Mother.

MARY:
>If it's not one, it's the other.

ROSIE: *calling*
What is it, Lonz?

ALONZO:
Would you get me a cup of tea, for the love of God.
Brad's burning, but I'm near froze to death.

> *WINSTON moves into the doorway.*

WINSTON: *disgusted*
Git it yerself. Jesus. I nivir saw the like of it.

ALONZO:
Now now, father, I learnt all me good habits from you,
remember?

WINSTON:
What I does is between yer mother and meself, and
don't ye fergit it. Ye always were too damned saucy.

> *BRAD suddenly leaps out of bed. He rushes to the
> window and looks out.*

BRAD:
Damned. We were all damned.

> *He stares at WINSTON, clutching the rum bottle.
> He rushes at him.*

Father, I beg of you. Throw that evil away.

> *He wrestles for the bottle. WINSTON easily shoves
> him back onto the bed, where he is about to fall
> on ALONZO. ALONZO, as he staggers, pushes him
> sideways.*

ALONZO:
Watch it.

BRAD: *pleading*
Father. Put that away.

51

WINSTON: *pointing at BRAD's crotch*
Ye put that away. I nivir knew ye'd got one.

ALONZO: *laughing*
The sword of the Lord out of its scabbard. A little
rusty, but ready for action.

> *BRAD, embarrassed, discomfited, backs to a chair,
> covering himself, then turns and begins to dress
> with great speed. WINSTON and ALONZO watch
> with interest.*

BRAD:
Why won't you listen. Why will nobody listen to me.
God.

> *He drops to his knees.*

God. Is this your will. Give me a sign, Lord. A sign.

ALONZO:
Who's he shouting at now?

WINSTON:
God knows.

SKIPPER:
I wants me rum. Me rum. Goddamn it, what's happenin'
in dis house this marnin'.

ROSIE: *shouting up*
Winston's on his way, Mr. Eli.

WINSTON:
Coming, Skipper. Coming.

> *He crosses to SKIPPER's bedroom, turns on the
> light and enters. The house is now ablaze. BRAD
> gets slowly to his feet and turns to face ALONZO.*

ALONZO:
> Nar sign, eh, Brad? Well, me son. Keep on trying, that's my motto.

BRAD:
> I feel sometimes as if I'm wrestling with the Devil.

MARY:
> The goings on in this house. It's disgusting, Rose. What must people think.

ALONZO: *interested*
> What's he like, Brad. I used to think he wor like a long lizard with a spiny tail.

ROSIE: *moving to the door with some tea*
> I 'lows it's too late to be t'inking of others now, maid.

BRAD:
> He's like you Alonzo. You.

ALONZO: *shaken by BRAD's intensity*
> Jesus. Yer as mad as the Skipper.

> *ROSE arrives in the doorway.*

ROSIE:
> Here you are, Lonz.

> *She hands the cup to him.*

ALONZO:
> Thanks, mother. Get me cigarettes, will ye. There . . . In me trousers . . .

> *He indicates the place his trousers are hanging. ROSIE obediently fetches them.*

ROSIE:
> Would ye like a cup of tea, Brad?

BRAD:
> I want nothing thank you, mother.

ROSIE:
> Ye got to eat and drink sometime, boy. Dey's hardly a t'ing to ye now. I got to fatten ye up.

ALONZO:
> The prodigal goose.

BRAD:
> Mother, no! I'm too upset. I have to pray. I feed on the Lord.

ROSIE:
> Well, if ye says so. Anyway I'll light the fire in the front room for ye. I knows how ye likes to be alone . . . Allus did, even as a youngster.
>
> *To ALONZO.*
>
> And ye leave off tormentin'n. Dey was quite enough o' dat last night!
>
> *She turns to go.*

BRAD:
> Mother.

ROSIE:
> Yes, Brad.

BRAD:
> Could you fetch my Bible for me. I think I left it in the front room.

ALONZO: *echoing WINSTON*
> Jesus. Git it yerself. Can't ye see she's run off her feet.

ROSIE:
> I'll git it the onct.

*The lights fade in their bedroom. WINSTON, in
SKIPPER's room, is pouring him a drink. SKIPPER
takes it, drains it with immense satisfaction and
holds the glass out for a refill.*

SKIPPER:
What were going on down there last night and this
marnin'?

WINSTON:
Oh nothing, Skipper. Celebratin' Good Friday, that's all.

*ROSIE re-emerges at the top of the stairs and
takes BRAD's Bible into him. She goes on out and
rests wearily in the shadow, listening to SKIPPER
and WINSTON, before going on down.*

SKIPPER:
Ah. That wor it then. I seen lots of 'em. Some good.
Some bad. They's places in the world where 'tis jest a
normal day.

*He pauses and drinks. A gust of wind shakes the
house. SKIPPER becomes intent, listening.*

Tell me, boy, is the war over yit?

WINSTON:
Not yet, Skipper. Not yet. Never will be, I reckon.

SKIPPER:
Bloody Germans. Hampering the seal fishery. Lost me
best barrelman last week . . . All the good hands gone
to be soldiers. Foolishness.

WINSTON:
Never mind, Skipper. Ye've still got a ship. And a crew.

SKIPPER:
Crew. They's wet behind the ears, me son. Frightened
o' me. Frightened o' wind and water, sick at the sight of
blood. Jump when they hears a swile bark. I 'ad better

eleven year old hands when I took me own schooner out
of Trinity, conning through the gut, the church rising
and falling behind, the bells ringin' . . . Women prayin'
to God to send we back . . . But not too soon . . . One-
eyed Bugden at the lookout. Tough as gads in them
days, boy! Are ye listenin'?

WINSTON:
> I hear ye, father.

> *He pours SKIPPER and himself another drink. The
> old man drinks, then sighs deeply.*

SKIPPER:
> That Kaiser. He must be some strange feller. Wears a
> gaff on his head I'm told.

> *Pause.*

> I tell ye, a man's enough to do fightin' nature. The rum,
> boy, the rum.

> *WINSTON fills his glass again.*

> Ye nivir did take to the salt water did ye, boy?

WINSTON:
> No, father. I can't say as I did. Too much work. Nothing
> but living gales and fog and no fish.

SKIPPER:
> Fish. Who cares about fish. Oh, they was necessary. On
> account o' them, we took to the salt water. An' we
> shovelled them into our guts till our blood were colder'n
> theirs. That were schoolin' ye might say, but the hunt,
> that's different. Every man, once in a lifetime, has to
> know what it's like. To hunt. To kill. To risk yerself,
> yer ship. Yer sons. Aye, and to lose sometimes.

WINSTON:
> Ye can do that at war, father. And ye can do it at 'ome,
> too!

56

SKIPPER:
> The hell ye can. It's not the same. Fightin' nature and
> fightin' yer brother . . . How kin that be the same?
> How old are ye now, boy?

WINSTON: *scratching his head*
> Fifty-eight, I 'lows. Or is it fifty-nine? Ye should know.

SKIPPER:
> Aye. I remembers. Two years afore yer sister. One afore
> yer brother, God rest his soul.
>
> *He pauses and drinks.*
>
> What makes a woman dry up like that . . . Like an ould
> cod.
>
> *Pause.*
>
> Did I do wrong, boy?

WINSTON:
> Ye didn't do anything, Skipper.

SKIPPER:
> Aye. That's right. Not fer any o' ye.
>
> *He lays back on the pillow with his eyes closed.*
>
> Cold seas. Cold land. Nothing growing. Only the harp,
> the whitecoat. Rust and blood and iron. No place fer a
> daughter. Shouldn't a made one. No place fer me, son,
> neither. Should we a made'n, Rachel? Should we?
>
> *Suddenly roaring.*
>
> I don't care if the wind has backed sou' east. Send the
> men over, damn you. Send them out. There's swiles to
> be killed. Ice to be trod. Out . . . Out . . .
>
> *He reaches for his stick and swings. WINSTON puts
> out a restraining hand.*

WINSTON:
Easy, Skipper. Easy, now.

SKIPPER glares, then comes back to normal.

SKIPPER:
Ach. Ye were always a disappointment to me, boy. But ye're human. Ye talk to me. Ye're mother now . . . Wunnerful fine woman, a comfort in me kitchen, aye, and me bed too. But she never talked. Not after yer brother died that time. Blamed me fer turnin'n out on the ice and steamin' off. But as God is me witness, I couldn't move. When the starm come it wor like the Divil had the ship in his hand. He wor a good man on the water. Better still on the ice. But he's gone now, along wi' the rest.

Pause.

Where's me gran'children? They's in the house. I heerd 'em. Bawlin' and shoutin'.

WINSTON:
Aye. They's in the house, Skipper. They'll be schoolin' around like the dogfish by'n by, but I wouldn't expect too much from 'em if I was you. One of 'em pretends ye don't exist and the other wants to save yer black soul.

He chuckles.

And the third waits fer yer will.

SKIPPER:
And what do ye want, boy?

WINSTON:
Nothing, Skipper. Ye knows that. Nothing at all. Jest this. A place to come and have a quiet drink, away from the women, and look out at the sea.

He gets up, takes a barometer from the wall and hands it to the SKIPPER. He moves to the chest of

*drawers. The top is littered with the SKIPPER's
medicine, old charts, a telescope. He picks up the
telescope and moves forward, looking out over the
sea. The storm sounds rise.*

SKIPPER:
What does she look like today, boy?

WINSTON:
Grey and ugly. Like an ould hag. They's some slob ice
be the look of it. But it's gittin' hard to see. They's a big
starm brewing I'd say.

> *SKIPPER taps the glass and studies it.*

SKIPPER:
Aye. The bottom's gone out of her. Twenty eight seven
and still fallin'.

WINSTON:
They's a small boat runnin' in now. Crazy fools. Nearly
too late to be the look of'n. She's down at the stern
and nearly awash. Jesus . . . She'll nivir get t'rough the
Barracks wi' that sea runnin'.

SKIPPER:
Ice boy. Any ice?

WINSTON:
I told ye. Some slob . . . Could be pack out there, but I
can't see the sea from the sky now . . . Christ, boys,
what are ye playin' at . . .

> *He turns.*

He's swinging back.

> *Unbelieving.*

He's going back out to sea!

SKIPPER:
After the swiles, boy. This is swile weather.

WINSTON:
I'd say he's after a quick trip to Hell . . .

He comes back and pours another drink for himself and SKIPPER.

SKIPPER:
Swiles is bred and killed in Hell, boy. Dis is their starm! The starm fer the young swiles! Oh, they'll love it. Swimming up in their t'ousands, looking for the pack ice to breed on. Fierce mothers, boy. Fierce and proud, I tell ye . . . And the young, helpless, floundering. But we be the same, boy, plunging and stumbling on the floes.

He starts to get excited.

It's their element, boy. Not ours. Our gaffs is their enemy. The nor' easter and the ice is our enemy. I tell ye, boy . . . I tell ye . . .

WINSTON:
Yes, Skipper . . . Ye tells me. All the time.

SKIPPER: *sitting back, quiet*
Ah, I thinks it's all gone at times. But ye never had anything to lose. Least, that's what ye thinks. And how could it be different when ye've done nothing but walk the shore all your life. But it isn't true for me, boy. They'll come back. The swiles'll come back in their t'ousands and when they do, I'll go greet 'em just like in the old days . . .

WINSTON:
What about yer legs, Skipper?

SKIPPER:
To hell wid 'em. I can crawl, can't I? That's what I did when I lost the use of 'em. When the ice took 'em. Is the house secure?

WINSTON:
Aye. Skipper. Mooring fast fore and aft.

SKIPPER: *to himself*
But not fer much longer I allows. Let me know when she starts to drag . . . How's the sea now?

WINSTON goes through the ritual again, crossing to the telescope, moving forward and peering out.

WINSTON:
Worse. Can't see nar thing. Nothin' alive out there . . .

SKIPPER:
The boat . . .

WINSTON:
She must 'ave gone. Must 'ave.

SKIPPER:
Aye, that's the way of it. Let me know when we starts to drift.

He is getting drowsy. He leans back on the pillow, clutching the barometer. WINSTON goes to him and takes the empty rum glass from the bed.

Send Rosie to me, boy. She knows how to comfort an old man.

WINSTON:
Knows how to comfort any man.

SKIPPER:
Makes ye tolerable, boy. Ye learned something after all. Ye picked a good ship. Steers herself . . . Makes no mind o' we and our foolishness.

He dozes. WINSTON begins to leave, quietly. SKIPPER, calling from the depths of his bed, says . . .

SKIPPER:
>Wake me when we gits to the field, boy. Don't ye fergit, mind!

WINSTON:
>Aye, aye, Skipper.

>*The sound of a hymn drifts up into the bedroom, "Eternal Father Strong to Save." SKIPPER sings the first two lines. The lights fade in the SKIPPER's room and go up on the kitchen as WINSTON comes down the stairs. MARY is sitting in the rocking chair and ROSIE is at the table finishing her breakfast. The SKIPPER's voice, keeping broken time with the hymn, drifts down softly. WINSTON enters as the ANNOUNCER breaks in.*

ANNOUNCER:
>We interrupt our broadcast to bring you a storm warning, just issued from Environment Canada in Gander. A disturbance to the East has deepened rapidly in intensity and is expected to bring storm force winds and a heavy snowfall to all parts of the island by midday. Marine interests are advised that severe storm warnings are now in effect for all Newfoundland waters. And now, before returning you . . .

>*WINSTON turns off the radio.*

WINSTON:
>According to the Skipper, 'tis the storm fer the young swiles.

>*He crosses to the day bed and lies down and stretches and yawns.*

>Rosie, love, fetch me a beer from the fridge, will ye.

MARY:
>Can't you see that she's having her breakfast. The poor woman hasn't stopped since she got up.

WINSTON:
Neither have you. More's the pity.

ROSIE:
Here ye are, love . . .

She hands him a beer and a hot bologna sandwich which she has collected from the oven on the way across.

Now eat up yer boloney, boy. Ye've got to soak up the liquor wid somethin' else ye'll nivir get t'rough the day.

WINSTON:
I'll do me best, maid, but it's a kind thought.

With one hand he swigs at the beer and with the other, he tries to get up ROSIE's skirt.

ROSIE:
Here you. Git your t'ievin' hands out of dat.

She swipes at him, pleased, and goes back to the table.

MARY:
Rose, I sometimes believe you encourage him deliberatel to keep the peace.

WINSTON: *exasperated*
Shut up, woman, fer the love of God before I say something I might regret. I've had a hard mornin' . . .

MARY sniffs.

Oh yis. Sneer all ye want. Talking to me father is always hard work, like reading hist'ry backwards. Yer own.

He leans back, subdued.

I wish sometimes that I could have been the son he wanted.

MARY: *vindictive*
Then you'd have been dead. Like Jacob.

WINSTON:
That's right, Mary.

He tips and drains the bottle.

That's absolutely Goddamn right.

MARY moves as if to speak, thinks better of it, and exits towards the livingroom. WINSTON, visibly upset, crosses to window and stares out. ROSIE keeps on eating, placidly.

Scene Three

The lights rise on the boys' bedroom. ALONZO is standing in his shirt and underpants looking out of the window, smoking. BRAD is sitting on a chair reading the Bible. His lips moving soundlessly.

ALONZO:
Hell of a day out there, Brad.

No response.

Bit like the night Mildred Tobin died.

No response.

I don't suppose ye'd care to remember that though. Always seemed to be able to block out things ye didn't want to remember.

No response. Disgusted, ALONZO comes down, stubs out his cigarette in the tea cup and gets his trousers.

D'ye mind when we left ye in the woods that time, fer a joke. Then couldn't find ye.

He laughs.

That were the time of yer first vision, weren't it? Though as I recall, it weren't God or the Virgin . . . The headless horseman, weren't it?

He struggles into his trousers. Annoyed at the indifference to his baiting, he crosses and looks over BRAD's shoulder. He declaims.

"Many times have they afflicted me from my youth, yet they have not prevailed against me." Heavy stuff, Brad.

No response. ALONZO loses his temper.

Brad, for God's sake, put that away and talk to me as a brother should.

BRAD:
Are you my brother, Alonzo?

ALONZO:
Ah ha. A voice. Out of the depths. More! More!

With a sudden movement he grabs the Bible from BRAD and throws it to the floor. BRAD rises and makes as if to strike him. ALONZO adopts a boxer's stance and prances round him.

That's it, brother. That's it. Do it, fer Christsake. Let's hurt each other like real people.

BRAD: *sitting slowly, retrieving the Bible and dusting it off*
You're not a real person, Alonzo. There aren't any real people in my family, apart from mother.

ALONZO: *crossing to him and willing BRAD into subjection*
Now listen, Brad. I've tolerated you ever since you were
a snot faced brat stealing quarters from me coat pocket.
I remember you.

> BRAD moves quickly to his feet, pushes past
> ALONZO with some force, and turns on him.

BRAD:
You listen. All my life I've been jeered at. That's all I
can remember. By stupid drunken men who were my
fathers or my brothers. And when they weren't drunk,
they hated me. Just for being alive. And now you jeer
at me for saying God is my father. Don't you think that
he's better than the one I've got?

ALONZO:
You mind yer mouth.

BRAD: *in an ecstasy of rejection*
And everyone here fearful, afraid to call on Him.
Catholic, Protestant, United . . . They're all the same.
Mumbling into prayerbooks. Sleeping in pews with
obscenities carved in the back of them. Trying to keep
God hidden. Like some dirty secret . . .

ALONZO: *shouting*
That's it. And that's all of it. I remember God help me,
when Mildred Tobin gave ye yer first and last piece of
tail. That were it, weren't it? Slobberin' and crying on
me shoulder, shouting out how ye was damned. Damned
foolish, that's what ye was, too stunned to use the
French safes I give ye. She poor bitch, led ye to God, or
whatever crazy thing it is ye've got in yer head.

BRAD:
You're an open sewer, Alonzo.

ALONZO:
Sewers are necessary, Brad. And don't fergit. It's your
shit I carry to the landwash, as well as me own.

66

BRAD:
> You don't have to lecture me. I'm responsible for myself.

ALONZO:
> Then keep to yerself and leave us alone to burn or freeze as we wish.

BRAD:
> I can't Alonzo. I have to learn . . . To love you.

> *The words are a release, an orgasm. BRAD takes a pace towards ALONZO, who backs away, unconsciously wiping his mouth with the back of his hand. BRAD recognizes a victory. He smiles. For a few moments his disintegrating soul is at rest.*

ALONZO:
> You're sick, Brad. Really sick.

> *ALONZO recovers his composure and eyes BRAD thoughtfully.*

> Tell me, what really happened up there? To yer flock? What did ye call yourselves . . . Oh yes, the Church of the Revelations.

BRAD:
> In the age of the Apocalypse, we are afflicted by many beasts.

ALONZO:
> Jesus!

BRAD:
> My congregation were led astray.

ALONZO:
> They couldn't've been that dumb after all. Must've seen ye were leading 'em to a God of blind alleys. I heard ye burnt out Joel Miller.

BRAD:
>Miller tried to corrupt my congregation. He was one of them. An agent of the Devil.

ALONZO:
>He was an agent for Labatt's. Fer Christsake, he ran a bar, that's all. A bar. Even Noah was allowed moonshine on the ark. Give me the book and I'll find the place for ye.

>*He snatches the Bible.*

>Father taught me that, years ago.

BRAD:
>The fire was an act of God.

ALONZO:
>Ye don't say. Well, 'twas nearly an act of murder. He were lucky to get out with just his face and hands burnt, to say nothing . . .

BRAD:
>There's no point in continuing this conversation, Alonzo. I've nothing to say to you.

ALONZO:
>I've noticed. But one thing puzzles me. Ye've been fired from the only job, if I kin call it that, that ye've ever had and ye come running back here. Why? Nobody wants ye.

BRAD:
>This is my home. This is where I began. Where we all began. That's right, isn't it? You were born in this room. Probably on that bed. And this is where we're going to die. All of us. You too, Alonzo.

ALONZO:
>Spare yer thoughts for the Skipper. It's his house. He might not like the idea of it being filled wit' corpses.

BRAD:
> Yes.

> *Pause.*

> I must see him. I must pray with him.

> *He crosses to the door and turns.*

BRAD:
> Alonzo, as it seems that we can't get on, would you leave me alone for the rest of the day. Please. For the sake of mother, if no one else.

ALONZO:
> A pact, is it? Like when we were kids. Alright then. Here . . .

> *He holds out his little finger. BRAD, searching his face, slowly holds out his. Just before the fingers touch and hook, ALONZO grabs for BRAD with his free hand with the intention of twisting finger and arm around. BRAD is too quick for him.*

> Ah, ye little bugger. Ye haven't forgotten, have ye?

> *BRAD, after a second, leaves to cross the landing. ALONZO shouts after him.*

> I wouldn't make a pact with you if it were the Day of Judgement.

BRAD:
> It is, Alonzo. It is!

> *WAYNE emerges on the landing from the stairs.*

WAYNE:
> Good morning, Brad. At it again, I hear.

BRAD ignores him and goes on into SKIPPER's
room. The old man is, or appears to be, asleep.
BRAD leans down, listens to his heart and nods.

BRAD:
Grandfather. Grandfather . . .

The old man doesn't stir. BRAD sits down by the
side of the bed, opens the Bible and begins to read
from the Book of Job. WAYNE has entered the
boys' bedroom. ALONZO is at the window. He
turns.

ALONZO:
D'you think Brad's queer?

WAYNE:
I don't know. I never slept with him.

ALONZO:
I can see ye're looking for more than a game of cards.
I thought ye were finished with us last night.

WAYNE:
Look, Alonzo. Let's face it. We don't like each other.
Never have.

ALONZO:
It's a morning of revelations. Now tell me, ye're learning
to love me.

WAYNE: *mocking*
I respect your ability.

ALONZO:
And I respect your position.

WAYNE:
I think you still owe me, Lonz.

ALONZO: *shaking his head*
Uh hunh. I deliver this district whenever it's required.
That's worth a lot.

WAYNE:
 And so is my survival.

ALONZO:
 Check. What do ye want?

 WAYNE sits on the bed, the sparring done.

WAYNE:
 It's about Grandfather.

ALONZO:
 You getting him committed.

WAYNE:
 It's possible.

ALONZO:
 What have I got to do with it?

WAYNE:
 I need your signature. Well . . . Not yours.

ALONZO:
 Father's?

WAYNE:
 That's right.

ALONZO:
 That's dangerous.

WAYNE
 You win some. You lose some.

ALONZO:
 You son of a bitch. Ye want me to forge the old man's
 signature in return for the motel contract.

WAYNE:
 I think I could guarantee it.

ALONZO:
> Think. Ye'd damn well better make sure of it if I'm
> going to forge the old man's signature. He'd kill the
> both of us if he ever found out.

WAYNE:
> He won't know. He'll never know.

ALONZO: *disturbed*
> Aunt Mary's been at ye, hasn't she? She's behind this.

WAYNE:
> Look. We're all worried about mother. How much more
> of this can she take.

ALONZO:
> The hell ye are. Christ!

> *He paces in agitation.*

> Will ye guarantee that contract? No delays. No bits and
> pieces. The lot.

WAYNE:
> I will.

ALONZO:
> Christ! What a bunch of rats we are. Have ye got the
> forms?

> *WAYNE takes them from the inside of his coat
> pocket. ALONZO takes them, scans them quickly,
> not wanting to read what they contain. He flips
> to the last page, takes the form to the chair and
> kneels, using the chair for backing.*

> Pen.

> *WAYNE passes him a gold pen.*

> Shit. Look at this.

He begins to scrawl, then looks up.

It's a long time since I've done this.

He scrawls.

There . . .

> *WAYNE takes the forms and puts them back in his pocket. ALONZO gets up.*

WAYNE:
Well, I suppose we'd better go and make the regulation visit. Get it over with. Are you coming?

> *ALONZO is staring at WAYNE.*

ALONZO:
I don't believe it.

WAYNE:
What?

ALONZO:
Doesn't matter. We'll go and pay our last respects. My arm . . .

> *He proffers his arm to WAYNE. The irony is lost on him. They cross the landing into SKIPPER's room. They both stay in the doorway. BRAD is intoning softly.*

BRAD:

Yea the light of the wicked is put out
And the flame of his fire does not shine
The light is dark in his tent
And his lamp above him is put out
His strong steps are shortened . . .

SKIPPER: *sitting bolt upright, roaring*
Miserable Comforter. What the hell do ye know about it. Get out. I'm not dead yet. Get out.

BRAD: *getting up a little hastily*
How are you feeling, Grandfather?

SKIPPER:
How do I look, ye fool. Better than ye do, I hope.

BRAD:
You're fading, Grandfather. You should be . . .

SKIPPER:
I'm not fading. What do ye think I am? A goddamned
flower? I'm dyin', ye pasty-faced pup. And I don't need
ye for company. It's hard enough as it is.

> *Pause.*

From the look o' ye, I judge ye to be 'Lonzo.

BRAD:
I'm Brad, Grandfather.

SKIPPER:
Ye all look and sound alike to me.

> *To himself.*

What happens to the roots? They isn't what they used
to be. So much rotten timber.

> *He calls out.*

Jacob . . . Jacob . . .

> *ALONZO, who has been delighted at this inter-
> change, comes in.*

ALONZO:
Well, Grandfather. Still around I see.

SKIPPER: *coming out of it with a start*
Ye're not Jacob. Get out.

ALONZO:
No, I'm not Jacob.

BRAD:
Jacob is dead, Grandfather. We must pray that he is
with God.

ALONZO:
Brad. Who cares? Leave the old man with his nightmares . .

SKIPPER:
Dead! Jacob, dead.

He is lost again.

Eighteen thousand and the decks awash with blood. It's
not enough, boys. Get over the side and to hell wid the
glass. Gaff and sculp . . . Gaff and sculp.

*There is another great gust of wind and a menace
in the silence that follows.*

ALONZO:
Aren't ye coming in, Wayne? Join the wake!

WAYNE: *advancing with his best politician's smile*
Grandfather. It's so good to see you.

SKIPPER:
Is it?

WAYNE:
Indeed, it is. And you're looking well too. You'll see the
lot of us out, as I've always said.

SKIPPER: *venomously*
I don't give a damn what ye've always said.

*He suddenly snatches up his stick and swings it
viciously. ALONZO manages to get out of its path
but it catches WAYNE squarely across the forearm.*

WAYNE:
My God.

He backs away staring at SKIPPER as if he were looking at the Anti-Christ.

Grandfather. You've broken my arm.

SKIPPER:
I should have had ye to the ice. Just onct.

He lashes out at the air with his stick.

Living off me. Grandchildren. Crackies more like. Not one o' ye a man. Not one of ye like Jacob. Ye've no God. And ye've no guts. Ye're nothin', the lot of ye.

He shouts.

Rosie . . . Rosie . . . Come and git yer whelps out of here. Rosie.

The lights partially rise downstairs. ROSIE is sitting eating, her mouth full of toast. WINSTON is standing looking out the window.

ROSIE:
What is it, fader?

WINSTON:
Fer the love of God, woman, leave him be. He's having a chat with the boys, that's all . . .

WAYNE:
We're going, Grandfather. We're going. Just came to pay our respects.

SKIPPER:
And that's about the only thing ye can pay.

WAYNE:
He doesn't know who I . . . Who we are obviously.

ALONZO:
> He knows, brother. He knows too well.

BRAD:
> I'll pray for you Grandfather . . .

SKIPPER: *roaring with rage*
> Curses, boy. I wants the curses of men. Not the piddlin' prayers of a mewlin' pup. I wants . . .
>
> *He glares about him in impotence, then sinks back, exhausted. BRAD leaves, clutching his Bible, and goes downstairs into the livingroom. WAYNE, holding his arm, turns to leave.*

ALONZO:
> Ye're not thinking of leaving.

WAYNE:
> No.

ALONZO:
> Good. I'd hate to be left without me thirty pieces of silver. I'll see ye later then.
>
> *WAYNE hesitates, then exits in the direction of his bedroom. ALONZO pokes about the room, finds the bottle of rum and pours himself a stiff drink. He sits down at SKIPPER's bedside. The old man makes a gurgling sound. ALONZO raises his glass.*

ALONZO:
> I knows ye don't mind, Skipper. Ye nivir did when I were a boy. Used to come up and read to ye. D'ye minds that. An' fer me birthday, ye'd allus give me a gold sovereign from out your chest. I've often wondered who ye'll leave that lot to. Mother, I 'lows. And the old man'll kill himself with the proceeds. Here . . .
>
> *He props him up with an arm and holds the glass to his mouth. SKIPPER drinks. ALONZO almost gently lays him back on the bed. He sits staring, eyes open.*

77

ALONZO:

> Ah, boy. Ye had your day. A good one too I allows if
> you're any recommendation. The times of the seal. But
> they've gone, Skipper. Gone, 'cept in your head and a
> few old log books. It's the day of the dogfish now.

> *He drains his glass and rises, placing the glass on
> the bureau. He goes out quietly. The lights fade
> and go up to full in the kitchen area. ROSIE is
> sitting having a cup of tea and toast, dipping her
> toast in the tea. WINSTON is standing downstage
> left looking out.*

ROSIE: *with her mouth full*

> What is it, love? What's the matter? Kin I get ye
> somethin'?

WINSTON:

> No, maid. No. Not just yet.

ROSIE:

> I knewed ye should have stayed in bed dis mornin'. Ye
> didn't look well . . . And yer stomach was grumblin'
> something awful . . .

> *She dips more toast. WINSTON speaks without
> turning, half to himself . .*

WINSTON:

> How long is it now?

ROSIE:

> What?

WINSTON:

> How long is it since we lost Sarah?

ROSIE:

> Oh my. Ye're t'inkin' o' dat agin, are ye?

78

WINSTON: *crossing to table*
> Every time I gits afflicted with me family I thinks of the one that might have been different. And Skipper don't help much.

ROSIE: *smiling*
> Aye. She wor a bonny thing. Not like me or ye at all. More like Grandmother Penton. Same colour eyes she had . . . And dat cow's lick atop her head. What ever would she have done wid her hair I wonder?

> *WINSTON hasn't heard.*

WINSTON:
> She might have had a chanct.

> *He turns to ROSIE.*

> I asked ye, Rosie. How long is it?

ROSIE:
> T'irty one years and two months. She'd have 'ad youngsters of her own be now. She wor borned in the February dark.

> *She pauses, struggling with memories and affection.*

> Ye minds how ye had to rush me to the hospital in the starm?

WINSTON:
> Aye, bundled ye up in the sled like an old walrus. And Trigger ploughing through drifts up to his chest. Like he knew . . .

ROSIE:
> I never seed ye like it. Ye were like a wild man. Like yer fader almost.

> *Proud.*

> I believe ye'd 'ave faced the Divil dat night and gone on.

She laughs.

ROSIE:
> The pains wor comin' every five minutes and the sled were rearin' from side to side, but I still minds ye cussin' . . . Trying to drive the snow away, I allow . . .

WINSTON:
> It wor never the same after she died. I doesn't know why. Once she'd gone, they wor . . .

> *He struggles painfully with the recollection.*

> I'd git into the woods and I'd see her, crouching in the snow, under the trees . . . And the damned foreman coming round charging ye five cents for every stump ye left in t'ree inches above ground. And me hacking away and not thinking, not thinking at all . . . Jesus!

ROSIE:
> I had to bind me breasts wit' oakum. I 'ad more milk for her and longer dan fer any of the boys. Still an all, the Good Lord saw how much we loved'n, and so He got a mite jealous I suppose . . .

WINSTON:
> The Good Lord! What's he got to do wi' us livin' and dyin'? To Hell wid'n.

ROSIE:
> Winston!

WINSTON:
> They's nothin', Rosie. Nothin'. They's madness and they's death and they's some who work at it and some who wait for it.

> *Brutally.*

> Sarey's out there and they's nothin' left of her save a peck o' dust.

ROSIE:
> Winston . . . Winston . . . It wor thirty years ago . . .

WINSTON:
> And two months. But it weren't, Rosie. It were today.

> *He crosses to exit.*

ROSIE: *upset and flustered*
> Winston, don't ye be goin' now like dat. I'll get ye a beer . . . Ye're upset . . .

WINSTON:
> No!

ROSIE:
> I cares for ye, Winston.

> *WINSTON stops by the entrance. He looks at her.*

WINSTON:
> I suppose ye do, maid. I s'pose ye do.

> *He laughs without mirth.*

SKIPPER:
> Rosie! Rosie!

WINSTON:
> And when he thinks I'm Jacob, so do he . . .

> *The lights fade.*

Act Two

ROSIE is attending the SKIPPER, tidying up the bed, rolling him from side to side with great speed and efficiency. Occasional curses spill from him, but they are not serious.

SKIPPER:
> Dammit, woman . . . Ye've got hands like a squid. D'ye think I'm a barrel of flour?

ROSIE:
> Dere now, Skipper . . . All done . . . How does dat feel?

SKIPPER:
> Terrible.

ROSIE:
> I knew ye'd feel better. Now it's time fer yer medicine.

SKIPPER: *roaring*
> I won't take it. I won't take it . . . I needs to capsize me cock.

ROSIE:
Ye've just done dat. 'Tis jest an excuse. Ye should be ashamed of yerself.

> *Impervious, she has gone to the chest of drawers, where she pours a liberal dose of evil-looking fluid into a small glass. SKIPPER struggles to slide down under the bedclothes, but thrashing and cursing is hauled up by ROSIE with one hand. He roars for the third time.*

SKIPPER:
Woman, I'm in charge of me own ship and she don't need none of that . . .

> *ROSIE seizes an opportunity when the toothless mouth is wide open and down the medicine goes. Sputtering and grumbling, SKIPPER swings at her with his stick, but she's already back at the cabinet and returns with a glass of rum.*

ROSIE:
I s'pose ye'll make me force dis down yer stubborn old t'roat too?

> *He glares, then chuckles and lays down the stick. He clutches the rum and lays back with a deep sigh of contentment.*

SKIPPER:
Ah, Rosie, Rosie. What a tumble we'd have had sixty years ago . . .

ROSIE:
Ye'd have been tumblin' by yerself, yer badminded ould divil . . . I weren't t'ought of den.

SKIPPER:
Oh yis, maid. Ye wor thought of. We've all got our own courses prepared long afore us gits here . . . The winds and currents waiting. The ships we meet. And the crews . .

ROSIE:
> Well now, I don't know not'ing about dat and I don't
> t'ink I wants to ... If ye're all settled ...

SKIPPER:
> No, Rosie. No. Don't go. Not yet. I wants ye to read to
> me.

ROSIE: *a little distracted*
> Ye've chosen a bad day fer dat an' me wit' a houseful
> downstairs.

SKIPPER:
> They's old enough to look after theirselves.

> *ROSIE pauses, irresolute, then she goes back to the
> chest of drawers. She opens a drawer, pulls out an
> old logbook, returns to the bed and sits in the
> rocker by the bedside.*

ROSIE:
> What day d'ye want?

SKIPPER: *with eyes shut*
> Aye, what day shall I have? There were that day in '19?,
> 18th March it wor ... Lost the cook. Crew gaffed him.
> Swore he wor pissin' in the stew.

> *He chuckles.*

> Tasted like it too. 30th March ... No. That's not the day
> I'm lookin' fer ... 5th April. Try that ...

> *ROSIE leafs through the ship's log and comes to
> the date. She begins to read.*

ROSIE:

> Log of the S.S. Bonavista. Master, Captain Elijah
> Blackburn, Trinity, Trinity Bay. Day dawned a bit
> mauzy. Glass dropping but not'ing to indicate real bad
> wedder. Big patch of swiles to the sout' east. Barrelman
> spotted anudder herd to the north. Sent half the men

over, wid Jacob Blackburn as Master Watch. We steamed
on into the mist. Looked back once to see how dey was
doing, a weak sun spilling t'rough a scad of snow. The
way dey was, so far away, dey seemed to form a t'in
black cross on the ice. Den the ground drift swallowed
dem up . . .

> *She stops reading and sits immobile in the chair.*
> *SKIPPER is crying great silent sobs that tear him*
> *apart. The light dims as we go downstairs to the*
> *kitchen. MARY is putting on her hat and coat,*
> *gloves, etc. She crosses to the bureau and takes*
> *down a Missal, checking herself in the mirror as*
> *she does so. Suitably impressed with her appear-*
> *ance before her Maker, she is about to depart when*
> *WAYNE comes through the door.*

MARY:
Wayne!

WAYNE:
Good morning, Aunt.

> *He comes in and kisses her on the cheek.*

MARY:
Did you sleep well?

WAYNE:
Like a baby. It was good of you to give up your bed.

MARY:
Oh, that's nothing. It's warmer downstairs after all. And
once your father had been dragged upstairs, it was quiet
enough . . .

> *The events of the past twelve hours have under-*
> *mined her reserves. She sits on the day bed, face*
> *averted, close to tears.*

WAYNE:
Aunt. Something's wrong.

He crosses quickly to her.

What's the matter?

MARY: *dabbing quickly at her eyes*
Oh, nothing. It's foolish of me to get so upset. Oh dear.
I see you so rarely, Wayne. I'm not used to . . . Kindness.

WAYNE:
Father's been at you this morning?

MARY:
He always is these days.

She rises.

I was just on my way to church.

WAYNE:
You can't go like that. Sit down for a moment, come
on.

*He leads her, vaguely protesting, to the rocking
chair.*

Now. I'll get you a cup of tea and then we'll go together.

MARY:
Oh, Wayne. Would you?

WAYNE:
We always used to.

He gets her cup of tea.

I still remember those summer mornings. We'd leave
early, just the two of us. You stopping to point out the
bank swallows, the terns. Steerings, we used to call
them. And I'd grab handfulls of wildflowers and grasses
from the roadside and you could identify every one.

MARY:
>
> Yes. Yes, I remember. There were some happy times then.

WAYNE:
>
> I owe a great deal to you, Aunt Mary.

MARY:
>
> Oh no, Wayne. You've repaid any debt a thousand times over.

WAYNE:
>
> It's not the kind of debt that can be repaid.

MARY:
>
> Wayne, I love to see you, you know that. But I wish you wouldn't come here. You don't belong here. That's what we worked for together, you and I, all those growing years. To free you from the cancer of this house, the horror of this place.

WAYNE:
>
> I know. But it disturbs me sometimes to think I've gained my freedom at your expense. Why don't you leave? Here am I, a bachelor with a huge apartment I can't run . . .

MARY:
>
> No, Wayne. I won't be a burden.

WAYNE:
>
> Burden? Aunt . . .

MARY:
>
> What could I do? I couldn't sit at home day after day waiting for you to get back. Oh, I know it's tempting. God knows, I lie awake at nights dreaming about it sometimes. But it would spoil, Wayne. I'd get to be like a nagging wife. I'm too old now. And I can teach here until I retire.

WAYNE:
I could get you a job in the school system in town.
There'd be no difficulty.

MARY:
Allow me some pride, Wayne. I'm not qualified. I
survive here because I'm something of an institution,
I suppose. And no one has the nerve to fire me. You do
help me you see, indirectly. Perhaps when father goes . . .

She pauses.

It might seem petty, Wayne. But I'm entitled to something from here. After all these years.

WAYNE:
I don't think justice is petty, Aunt. And that's all you're
asking.

*It is a moment of complete sympathy and bonding
between them. She hands WAYNE her cup. He
takes it and puts it on the table.*

WAYNE:
D'you know Grandfather hit me this morning.

MARY:
What?

WAYNE:
Well. You did warn me in your last letter. I got a bit too
close to that stick of his, that's all.

MARY:
The old savage. Are you alright?

WAYNE:
Oh yes. Just a bruised arm. I think he'd like to have
done more damage than he did.

MARY:

I'm worried, Wayne. What if he struck your mother one day in one of his fits. He doesn't know where he is or who he's talking to half the time.

WAYNE after a moment checks the entrance to stairs and pauses a moment at the livingroom door. He comes back to MARY and lowers his voice.

WAYNE:

I've good news for you, Aunt. That's the main reason I'm here. I've spoken to the Health and Welfare people. We can get him into a home by making a case for psychiatric treatment.

MARY:

Psychiatric treatment!

Hope flares up in her.

Wayne, there can't be any doubt. He's been living in the past for so long, I swear sometimes he believes that we're all crew members on his wretched boat.

Pause.

Will it take long?

WAYNE:

I think we can get him off your hands within the week.

MARY:

A week! Wayne . . . Wayne. I knew you wouldn't let me down. You've never let me down. But are you sure? What do we have to do?

WAYNE:

Now don't you bother your head with the details. You've quite enough to worry about.

MARY:
> Oh, I'm so excited! I should be sorry — or ashamed — but all I can feel is relief. Oh, I do my best to keep up appearances but it's so difficult. And the people have got such a respect for him when it's you they should be proud of. I heard you were in line for a Cabinet post. Is that true?

WAYNE: *laughing*
> So much for Cabinet secrecy.

MARY:
> Then it is true.

WAYNE:
> Murdock's retiring next month on the grounds of ill health. He's really being fired for inefficiency. You're looking at the next Minister of the Environment.

MARY:
> Wayne. I'm delighted for you.

WAYNE:
> And I am delighted for you. With grandfather in a place where he can be properly looked after things might change a little round here. Why you might even be able to finish your marking.

> *He crosses to the day bed, picks up a loose book and thumbs through it.*

WAYNE: *laughing at her gently*
> Let's see if you've changed your style. No. No. Nothing has changed. Do you remember how you trusted me to mark the grades beneath mine. Severe but fair. Those were your instructions. I've never forgotten them.

> *MARY crosses to him, takes his hands.*

MARY:
> You're right, Wayne. Things will be different. Perhaps I could come down for a weekend or two. Then you wouldn't need to come back here at all.

She pauses.

MARY:
Wayne. Can I ask you something?

WAYNE:
Surely.

MARY:
You're doing something for Alonzo again, aren't you?

WAYNE:
Well . . . It's something of mutual benefit, Aunt.

MARY:
Be careful, Wayne. Alonzo has designs upon you, I know it. He's clever. And without scruples.

WAYNE:
He's a bit of a crook, I know. But he does organize the party in this district and I have no choice but to work with him on occasions . . .

MARY moves to interject, but he cuts her off.

You're right, Aunt. But don't you worry. I can handle him. Now . . .

He proffers his arm.

Shouldn't we be going?

ROSIE bustles in.

ROSIE:
My, Wayne. You're the first down! Lord knows what the udders is doing. Have ye 'ad somet'ing to eat?

WAYNE:
No, mother. As a matter of fact, I'm just on my way to church with Aunt Mary.

92

ROSIE:
Ye can't go out in dis widout a bit o' somet'ing in yer stomach. And jest look at ye, ye're not dressed fer the Divil wettin' his mudder an' it blowin' a livin' starm out dere. Now, ye sit down here . . .

She bustles him protesting to the table.

An' 'ave a nice cup o' tay whiles I gits ye a bit o' fish.

WAYNE clutches his stomach.

Would ye like a drop o' rum in yer tay, das if yer fader's left any?

She scurries rapidly to the stove with a plate, dollops a handsome portion of fish and brewis on it and thrusts it in front of him just as he is trying to rise.

WAYNE:
Mother. Really. I couldn't . . .

He turns an appealing face to MARY.

MARY:
I'm afraid your mother believes all men to be carbon copies of your father.

ROSIE:
Carbon or not, yer not goin' out widout somet'ing and dat's dat. Whatever would dey say in St. John's if ye got sick out here, an important man like ye?

WAYNE: *desperately*
Mother. Just the look of that makes me feel sick. Now take it away! Please!

MARY:
Wayne . . . We must be going. It will be a hard walk in this weather.

She comes and takes one arm.

93

ROSIE:
> Now, Mary . . . He's not leaving until he's at least 'ad a cup o' tay.

> *ROSIE grabs his other arm.*

MARY: *tugging firmly*
> It's time our little church was honoured with the presence of its most famous son. Surely Rosie, you, his mother, would agree to that.

ROSIE: *tugging him the other way*
> And what if he faints wid hunger as dey're taking up the collection . . . Some proud we'd be den, I 'lows.

WAYNE: *finally breaking clear of them both and going centre*
> Please . . . Please . . . Both of you!

> *He inspects his suit for damage.*

> Look, don't you think it would be better if we went in the car? I have studded snow tires. It shouldn't be too much of a problem.

MARY: *pleased*
> Why, Wayne! How nice of you. It's a long time since I had a ride in a car. Well, in that case, you do have time for something.

> *WAYNE is about to protest, but MARY puts a restraining hand on his arm.*

> Rose. Stop fussing. You've got quite enough to take care of. Wayne, you sit down there . . .

> *Proferring the rocking chair.*

> And here's your tea . . .

> *She deftly evades ROSIE and gets the poured tea from the table.*

Now . . . What would you like?

WAYNE:

Some lightly scrambled eggs please, with just a little milk. Doctor's orders, I'm afraid . . . My ulcers.

ROSIE: *taking the fish and brewis from the table and pouring it splashily back into the pot* My, Wayne, you got ulcers? Uncle Jim Tobin had one o' dem last year. Or wor it two? Just afore 'e died. Terrible pain 'e wor in . . . Bleeding like a pig inside.

WAYNE winces.

Leastways, dat's what Aunt Sadie said, but I always reckoned it wor 'is conscience dat killed'n fer driving poor Mildred out of the house. And her only one hour from borning the baby.

MARY has doffed her hat and gloves and Missal, putting them back on the bureau. She takes off her coat and, laying it on the day bed, starts to prepare WAYNE's scrambled eggs.

MARY:

Uncle Jim may have been severe, Rose, but he was morally right.

To WAYNE.

His own niece now. Everyone knew. Carrying on on the day bed while he was upstairs praying for Winifred, God rest her soul.

ROSIE: *stubborn*

It were a wicked t'ing she done, I allow, dough God knows the fellers she done it wit' is alive and well enough to sing the Lord's praise on the Sabbath and nobody minds dat.

MARY:
It's the girl's responsibility to keep herself pure. Until marriage at least. What do you think, Wayne?

ROSIE:
What do he know about it. Men are all alike when it comes to dat an' I suppose dey's no harm in it in the long run.

MARY:
That's a matter of opinion. I'm sure if Wayne had spent his college days running around after every loose girl he wouldn't be where he is now.

ROSIE:
Jest the same, I wish I'd a knowed. It blowin' a starm jest like today and cold as a drowned man's breat'. And she desperate and shamed into crawling under Winston's old punt.

MARY: *grim*
Aye, and because of that bit of stupidity the tongue waggers pointing at Winston for the father as if we didn't have enough trouble already.

ROSIE: *reliving her emotions, her compassion struggling for expression* I don't care if Winston wor or worn't. I doubts it dough, the liquor had him slowed down a bit even afore you, Wayne.

MARY:
Rose. Does he have to be reminded of those things? There you are, Wayne.

She hands him his scrambled eggs.

ROSIE:
We all needs to be reminded of some t'ings, maid. And t'were a terrible way to die in a place where we're all kin. Baby boy it were. The pair of 'em frozen together until Winston found 'em when the ice cleared

in the spring. If only she'd 'ave come 'ere. Ye was in St. John's den, Wayne. At the University. Ye minds dat? I wrote and told ye. Ye was sweet on her one time I remember, used to follow 'er home from school.

She laughs at the memory.

But she were a wild one dat, I remembers . . .

MARY: *getting irritated by ROSE's reminiscences*
For goodness sake, Rose. Christian charity is one thing, sloppy sentiment is another. She got her just desserts.

As she speaks, there is a howl of wind, a door opening and slamming at the side entrance left. WINSTON appears carrying a dozen beer, stamping the snow off his boots and shaking himself. He is in by the last line.

WINSTON:
Here Rosie, get me coat, will ye?

She scurries across and helps him off with it. She disappears into the passage left.

Christ! The things a man has to do to get a dozen beer on a public holiday.

He crosses to the fridge and begins to stack in the beer.

Who got her just desserts, Mary? What poor soul are ye tormentin' this time?

ROSIE comes back on.

ROSIE:
Mildred, dear. Mildred Tobin . . . Ye remember.

WINSTON:
I'm not likely to forget, am I?

He uncaps a beer and, still by the fridge door, takes a satisfying swallow.

WINSTON:
> And I suppose the baby did, too, eh? Breath enough for one cry before the air froze in his throat. I reckon he got his just desserts. Or should we be thankful that God took him back before more harm could befall the little bugger?

> *He has wandered into the main area and crosses in front of WAYNE.*

> Good morning, son. I hardly recognized ye. What in the name of God are ye eating?

WAYNE:
> Oh, good morning, father. Scrambled eggs.

> *WINSTON is interested. He swivels around, grabs the plate and looks at the remains.*

WINSTON:
> Scrambled. I thought that only happened with brains.

> *He hands WAYNE back the plate.*

> What do ye do? Smash 'em up with a fork and fry 'em? Looks like baby shit to me.

MARY:
> Do you always have to be so crude?

WINSTON: *shouting*
> Yes, by God. Because I am crude. I drinks because it helps me to fergit where I am and I swears because I like it. It sounds good and it protects me from your kind of literacy. And I likes jokes about natural functions because they're funny and they're particularly funny when aired in front of ye. I suppose ye've never farted in yer life. What is it ladies do, break wind?

> *He laughs.*

I can see ye now, catching it and bending it over yer knee and trying to tan its little arse off . . .

He laughs again.

What do you think of that, son?

MARY:
If only the child were the father of the man.

She takes WAYNE's plate.

WAYNE:
Then I could wish my days to be bound each to each by natural piety.

MARY: *delighted*
You haven't forgotten.

WINSTON:
Jesus. I've sired a book of sayings.

He takes a swig.

Well, son . . . Now that ye've finished yer scrambled eggs I wants to ask you a question. How's the government?

MARY:
Wayne . . .

She hurries to the chest of drawers and once again attires herself in her church accessories.

We really should be going now.

WAYNE:
Right.

WAYNE rises from the rocker, but is suddenly thrust back as WINSTON turns and forces him down with one hand.

WINSTON:
It's not alright. I'm asking ye a question, son, and I wants an answer. Don't see ye very often. Ye can talk to God any day of the week, like the Virgin Mary there, but it's not often ye gets a chance to talk with yer father.

MARY:
Thank God for small mercies, Wayne. I don't have such luck.

WAYNE: *rising again, and managing it, but keeping a wary eye on WINSTON* I'm sorry, father, but I promised Aunt Mary I'd run her to church. I'll be right back . . . We can chat over lunch.

WINSTON: *stares at him in disbelief*
Chat! Over lunch!

ROSIE:
Heard your name on the radio yesterday, Wayne. Just afore ye arrived. It said ye'd sold somet'ing to the Japanese.

WAYNE: *moving towards MARY*
That's right, mother. The last fifty thousand acres of standing timber to the Nippon Match and Transistor Company. I don't mind telling you, it was tough going.

WINSTON:
What're they going to use it for, matches or transistors?

WAYNE:
That's only the name of the parent company. They're global now, oil, shipping, newsprint. This province is the only one in Canada whose economy is on the upswing.

WINSTON:
I'm not interested, son.

He suddenly swings up and spins around WAYNE.

100

Whether you've sold yer arse to the Japanese. I am interested in the Welfare. Now. When is that crowd yer with going to do something about increasing it? Ye don't get my vote until ye do. And that would be a terrible thing, son, for the press to discover.

He reads from an imagined newspaper.

Mother and father vote for son's political opponent. "He's neglected us for years," said pale-faced Mrs. Rosie Blackburn, clutching a five year old to her empty dug. Ever since we put him through college when me husband developed heart trouble from overwork!

WAYNE:
Father, I already send you a considerable allowance on top of your social assistance. And I'm taking a risk doing that.

MARY:
Wayne. You know he's only goading you. Come along now. We're going to be late.

WINSTON dodges between WAYNE and MARY.

WINSTON:
Ye do send us a piece of yer travelling expenses I know, and yer mother and I are very grateful, aren't we, Rosie?

ROSIE:
Oh yis, I don't know what we'd do widout it, the price of liquor being what it is.

WINSTON:
Things is going from bad to worse in this house, son, because yer aunt hides all her money and try as I might, I can't find it. And I haven't got the heart to take anymore from me father.

MARY:
What I do with my money is none of your business, Winston Blackburn. I earn it, d'you hear. By work.

101

MARY:
> It's mine. Mine! And I'm saving it to keep the rest of us alive when you've drunk yourself into a beery grave.

> *WAYNE puts a restraining hand on her arm.*

> I swear, Wayne, that if he could forge my signature at the bank, every penny of it would have been gone long ago.

> *ALONZO comes downstairs and through the centre door into the scene.*

ALONZO:
> Good morning, all. What a lovely Good Friday this is.

> *He goes to his mother and gives her a swing which drops her breathless.*

> My God, mother. You're getting broad in the beam.

ROSIE:
> Yis, boy, and ye helped make it dat way. Git on wid ye now.

> *She pushes him away and, taking a pot from the stove, moves into the pantry area. He follows her.*

ALONZO:
> It's an amazing household ye run, mother. Brad's been reading the Bible now fer the past hour, Skipper's loaded, and the rest of the family's plotting to send each other to the funny farm.

WAYNE:
> Alonzo!

ALONZO:
> Easy, brother. Don't strain yer ulcers. Ah mother, if only I could begin to describe to ye the glow of goodness that fills me breast on this day of days. Ye see in me, mother, a new man.

MARY:
Mph. The Good Lord had better watch the patent.

ALONZO swings round, advances on MARY and grabs her hands.

ALONZO:
Aunt Mary, by all that's holy. You look as ravishing as ever. Why has no one ever sought to suck the honey from those sweet lips. Drown in those pools of blue, lay his tired head upon that gentle breast . . .

MARY throws off his hands.

MARY:
Wayne. I'm leaving this instant.

WAYNE crosses to MARY and takes her arm.

ALONZO:
No ye don't, brother. Not yet. We've business to discuss and time is running out. I've got to be gone be dark.

WAYNE:
We'll talk later, Alonzo. When I get back from church.

ALONZO: *reading his mind*
We'll talk now I think, Wayne. I knows what's on yer mind. Ye're aiming to slip off to church and then barrel off back to town or wherever it is you're going. Aunt Mary kin find her own way to Salvation. Ye stay put.

He grabs WAYNE by the arm, the bruised arm. WAYNE gives a yelp of pain and with a reflex action strikes out at ALONZO. ALONZO prances round him and hits him in the midriff, catching him off balance and knocking him down. He crouches in boxer style, both fists at the ready.

Come on then. If that's the way ye want it. Come on.

MARY: *almost in tears*
Wayne!

WINSTON:
One, two, three, four, five . . . Rosie, maid, this is better entertainment than TV.

WAYNE rises with murder in his soul. For an instant it looks as if he's about to give battle. ROSIE pushes between them.

ROSIE:
Fer the love of God, boys, give over dis foolishness.

WINSTON:
Sock it to 'em, Rosie.

WAYNE:
There'll be no contract, Alonzo. I can promise you that.

ALONZO:
Oh yes there will, brother. Haven't ye forgotten something? Father . . . I got something to tell ye.

WAYNE: *reverting to origins*
By Jesus, 'Lonz. I'll take you with me.

They square off. Again, ROSIE pushes them apart.

ROSIE:
Nobody's taking nobody nowhere, 'cepting Wayne. Now, boy, ye take Mary off to church afore dere's any more trouble. And ye.

She turns to ALONZO.

Ye mind yer manners. Dis is still my house and I'm not above giving ye a tanned arse.

ALONZO:
What about it, Wayne?

WAYNE:
    I'll be back.

    He and MARY move to exit. ALONZO prances
    after them.

ALONZO:
    I've just lost me stripper down to the Blue Flamingo,
    Aunt Mary. Me and the boys was wonderin' whether ye
    was any good with a bottle.

MARY:
    Rose. I won't set foot in this house again until I have an
    apology from that brothel keeper there.

    Mustering the remnants of dignity, she and
    WAYNE sweep out.

WINSTON: *calling out*
    Is dat a threat or a promise?

    A great gust of wind. The door slams. ALONZO,
    laughing, turns and shuts the door. He is greeted
    with a stinging slap on the face from ROSIE.

ALONZO: *startled*
    Jesus, mam. What was that fer?

ROSIE:
    Ye knows. And ye'll git anudder if ye keeps up like dat.
    I'm well able fer ye and don't ye ferget it. Yer poor
    Aunt. She's been driven right crazy dis marnin' by yer
    fader. And ye spoils the one chanct she gits to see
    Wayne.

    With unconscious irony.

    An' she been like a mudder to'n.

    ALONZO, a little subdued, goes down into the
    pantry area and sits.

105

ALONZO:
> Oh come on, mother. If Mary hadn't got anything to be
> disgusted about, she'd commit suicide.

WINSTON:
> Drive some poor kid in school to suicide more like.

> *ALONZO begins to examine the plates on the
> table.*

ALONZO:
> Mm! What have we here . . . Fat back . . . Fish and brewis,
> herring . . . My God, mother, you've excelled yerself . . .
> I can see I'll have to get married.

WINSTON:
> I heard ye had . . . Widout the benefit of clergy. Several
> times . . .

ALONZO: *sardonically*
> They's not too many women like mother around any
> more, father. They don't seem to want to put up wi' it
> somehow.

ROSIE: *sadly*
> It'd be so nice if one o' ye would at least. I 'lows if
> Sarah 'ad been alive we'd a had some grandchildren of
> our own be now.

SKIPPER:
> Winston . . . Winston.

WINSTON: *impatient*
> What is it now?

> *Under his breath.*

Jesus.

SKIPPER:
> Winston.

106

WINSTON: *resigned*
Aye, Aye, Skipper.

SKIPPER:
She's slipping her moorings, son. Git up on the bridge.

WINSTON:
Don't be so foolish, Skipper. She's fine.

BRAD has entered silently.

SKIPPER:
Be the Lar' liftin' Jesus. Haul yer arse up on that bridge afore I . . .

WINSTON:
Alright, Skipper. Alright.

ALONZO:
He's in a bad way this morning.

WINSTON crosses to the fridge for another beer. ROSIE bustles out through the door and leaves it open.

WINSTON:
He's been in a bad way every morning this past twenty years.

He turns to go up, pausing to swig from the bottle. He sees BRAD.

My God! It's the second coming. Again!

BRAD:
You shouldn't do that, father.

WINSTON:
What?

BRAD:
You shouldn't encourage him. It's not good for him.

WINSTON stares at him, amazed. BRAD gains courage.

BRAD:
> He's living in the past instead of getting ready to meet God. That's not good for anyone. He's dying and you're destroying his soul. With that.
>
> *He points at the bottle.*
>
> As well as your own.

WINSTON:
> Oh. I am, am I?

BRAD:
> YES.

WINSTON: *advancing on BRAD*
> Let me tell you something, son. I encourage him because it's all he's got. Because his dreams mean more to'n than what's left of his children. That's me and yer Aunt, son, if you gits me meaning. And they mean a damn sight more to him than his grandchildren do, including ye, with or without yer collar.
>
> *He moves away and turns back.*
>
> And I'll tell ye something else. I encourage him because beneath that wrinkled old skull and those mad eyes I kin sometimes see a truth about meself which might make some sense out o' dying. D'ye understand. Killing him! Christ!
>
> *ROSIE appears in the doorway with an armful of splits. She puts them in the woodbox.*

ROSIE:
> Ye see, Brad, for yer fader, it's a way o' getting out of the house.

WINSTON: *laughing*
> Rosie, Rosie, wiser than us all . . .

ROSIE:
'E'll need a drop o' water now fer 'is toddy.

She gets a small jug and fills it.

BRAD:
You're as bad, mother.

He restrains her.

Can't you see that? Are you frightened of them? Are you? I'm not. Oh, they can humiliate me. They can laugh at me. But God . . . Yes, God has made me strong this morning. He'll help me to make you strong.

ROSIE: *upset*
I doesn't know what ye're on about, Brad.

BRAD:
What do you think is going to happen when father and grandfather, and yes, Alonzo too, stand before God in all His glory, stinking of rum. It is today, mother. Today. Listen. Listen to the Voice of the Angels.

BRAD has worked himself up into a pitch of fervour. His is not true insanity, but the glorification of a mutilated ego as narrow as it is intense. Clothed in the richness of his fantasy, in the words of revelation, he becomes at this instant, radiant, superior, his words imbued with an impact beyond his own fragile identity. He is The Messenger and even WINSTON and ALONZO are spellbound confronted by this immolation of the spirit.

Babylon is fallen, is fallen, that great city, because she made all nations drink of the wine of the wrath of her fornication. If any man worship the beast and his image and receive his mark on his forehead or in his hand, the same shall drink of the wine of the wrath of God which is poured without mixture into the cup of his indignation and he shall be tormented with fire and brimstone in

109

the presence of the Holy Angels and in the presence of the lamb. And the smoke of their torment ascendeth up forever and ever and they shall have no rest . . . Day or night!

There is a hushed pause.

BRAD:
Mother. Come with me.

WINSTON:
She won't be going, Brad.

ROSIE senses an assault.

ROSIE:
'Tis alright, Winston. He wor always like dis. Me fader wor much the same. There wor no one like God to his way o t'inking.

WINSTON: *ignoring her*
I won't be there neither. In fact, I've no intention of going in front of Him at all if I kin 'elp it. I nivir took to the idea of bein' surrounded by a bunch o' damn fairies singing hymns day and night.

ALONZO:
Heave it out o' ye, father.

BRAD:
That's blaspheming, father.

He is still riding the power of a few moments ago.

Your soul is burning.

WINSTON:
Feels like heartburn to me, son. An' what ye calls blasphemy I calls common sense. Nivir could stand that nonsense, 'Lonz, even as a young feller. All them damned fairies bursting their little hearts out blowing

the last trump. Like a Billy Graham revival hour. When I goes, I'll go wit' what I knows. An' that's nothing, boy. D'ye hear. Nothing.

BRAD:
Ye see, mother. He's lost. He's doing it deliberately.

WINSTON:
You're damn right I'm doing it deliberately. Which is more I kin say fer ye when I spawned ye. Rosie, I half blames ye. Ye nivir fed me enough that night. Jesus. If I started to tell the Good Lord what I t'inks o' ye, 'twould fill the Book o' Judgement.

BRAD with a swift movement takes ROSIE's hands and slowly brings her to her knees.

BRAD:
God, in your infinite kindness look down upon this wretched house and see that there is one yet who is pure of heart, whose sins are of omission only, Lord . . . Of love. Spare her Lord. Spare her!

ROSIE, confused and upset, is in tears. She struggles to release BRAD's grip, but WINSTON, outraged, moves swiftly and throws BRAD sprawling.

WINSTON:
Ye leave yer mother be. An' if I wor ye, I wouldn't be so anxious to get to them pearly gates, because ye knows who'll be waitin' fer ye.

BRAD: *shouting, frightened at the violent intensity of WINSTON's anger* God. God will be waiting.

WINSTON:
God! No, b'y. Mildred Tobin. Wit' that poor little bastard of hers still froze to her tit. And what will ye say to that, ye snivellin' gospeller.

111

BRAD: *wavering*
That's between me and God.

WINSTON:
Oh it is, is it?

ROSIE:
Now, Winston. Ye don't know that he wor the fader fer sure.

WINSTON:
I've allus knowed. I heard a conversation between him an' 'Lonz the night after he done it. Book o' Judgement.

He stands over BRAD.

Ye might be a true disciple now me son, but don't fergit yer mother and I remember the shape and colour of yer arse.

He half lifts then throws BRAD across the room where he crashes into the wall.

ROSIE:
Winston!

WINSTON:
Git out. I don't want ye in my house. Git out.

BRAD:
God, help me. Help me.

In the brief silence, only the howl of the storm is heard.

ALONZO: *soft*
They's nobody out there, Brad. They's only us.

BRAD:
Mother . . . I've nowhere to go.

112

WINSTON:
Then go to Hell and keep a place fer me.

*WINSTON moves as if to assault him again, but
ROSIE gets between them.*

ROSIE:
Don't be mindin' yer fader, Brad. Ye knows what he's
like when 'e's 'ad a few.

She wipes her eyes with her apron.

I don't know what's happenin' in dis house dis day.
Everyone at it like cats an' dogs. I wish . . . I wish we
could all sit down like we used to an' sing a bit an'
laugh . . .

WINSTON: *savage*
We nivir laughed, woman. Stop coddin' yerself. And fer
the love o' Jesus, will ye stop motherin' that. Let'n go
and crawl out under me ould punt. Might be some
justice in that.

BRAD:
I didn't know! Christ believe me.

He is sobbing.

I didn't know.

WINSTON:
Well, ye knows now. And it's time ye kept that picture
in front of ye, son. Instead of a God ye've invented to
please yerself and a book ye don't understand. And
when ye learns just what ye are, ye might be more of
a man than ye've ever shown yerself to be in this house.

*He crosses to the stove and picks up the jug of
water where ROSIE has left it.*

WINSTON:
This water's cold, woman.

He exits upstairs. ROSIE kneels to comfort BRAD.
He grabs at her.

ALONZO:
> That's told ye, boy. Ye should have listened to me this
> marnin'.

ROSIE:
> Ye keep yer big mout' out o' dis. Ye've done enough
> harm fer one day, God knows.

ALONZO:
> Me?

BRAD:
> He hates me.

ROSIE:
> No, b'y.

> *She comforts him.*

> Yer fader don't hate nobody. He's a good man. 'E
> would've liked somet'in' better fer all of us, but dat's it,
> I suppose.

BRAD:
> Do you love me, mother?

ROSIE:
> Dat's a foolish question.

BRAD:
> No, it isn't. You never told me.

ROSIE: *hurt and confused, she releases BRAD and gets up*
> Brad. Ye always makes me feel so guilty. I means, ye
> don't talk about what's dere.

ALONZO:
> Leave her alone, Brad.

114

He moves protectively to ROSIE.

They was never any love here, sure. Not the kind o' thing your looking fer anyways. We was too busy survivin' to put up with any o' that old foolishness.

> *BRAD gets up and for one stricken moment looks from one to the other, then suddenly hurls himself from the room. There is the bang of the outside door. ROSIE rushes after him.*

ROSIE:

Brad. Brad . . . Ye come back 'ere. Brad . . .

> *The storm shakes the house. ROSIE re-enters. She is at the breaking point.*

'E's gone out now, widout not'in' on, no coat nor boots, not'in'. He'll perish sure.

> *ALONZO crosses to her and puts his arm about her shoulder.*

ALONZO:

Don't worry about'n, mother. He'll not do anything foolish.

ROSIE:

But it's so bad. It's so bad.

> *She crosses and sits in the rocking chair, closing her eyes.*

'Lonz. Git me a cup o' tay, will yer?

ALONZO: *surprised*

What . . . Are ye sick, mother?

> *Nonetheless he rapidly gets her a cup of tea.*

ROSIE:
I dunno, b'y. Tell ye the trut'. The stomach's left me. Everyt'in' seems to be gone . . . Or going . . . Somehow.

She sips her tea and rocks.

Turn the radio on would ye, 'Lonz. Dere's a good boy. Dere might be a nice hymn or two playing to cheer me up.

ALONZO turns on the radio and the last verse of "Amazing Grace" played by the Pipe Band of the Royal Scots Greys swells out. It has the cadences and the implication of a dirge for the fallen.

ALONZO goes and sits in the pantry area, picking up a paper from the top of the cupboard as he does so. He sits and reads as the lights dim in that area. They remain on ROSIE while the hymn plays. She is sitting back, eyes closed, rocking slightly. The tears fall down her cheeks.

The lights fade to black as the band falls silent. Suddenly, there is a crackle of static and into the blackness a rather panicky ANNOUNCER says . . .

ANNOUNCER.
We interrupt our program to advise all listeners that a state of emergency has been declared and . . .

A crackle of static.

All communications with the mainland have been disrupted and difficulty is being . . .

A crackle of static.

R.C.M.P. advise that no vehicles may be operated except . . .

A crackle of static.

Power disruptions may be expected and residents are . . .

There is more static which fades off into a low hum and then out. From this moment on the radio remains on, fading off and on as the power flows intermittently. The lights go up slowly in the SKIPPER's room as WINSTON enters. They are at about half power.

WINSTON:
Master Watch reporting for duty, Skipper.

SKIPPER:
Master Watch. Jesus, b'y. Ye'd nivir have made second cook on my ship.

WINSTON:
I wouldn't 'a made that on me own neither.

SKIPPER:
Listen, boy. Listen.

The storm howls.

WINSTON:
'Tis bad enough alright. Not fit fer man or beast . . .

SKIPPER:
Listen, I tell ye!

Silence. Again, the storm howls. It is very eerie . . . Like a voice out of the elemental past.

Did ye hear it that time?

WINSTON:
The wind, that's all.

SKIPPER:
No, b'y. A swile. They's a swile out there.

WINSTON:
Can't say as I heard him, Skipper.

SKIPPER: *sighing*
Are we fast, boy?

WINSTON:
Aye. Fast enough. Couldn't shift her wi' dynamite.

SKIPPER: *sitting bolt upright*
I said that. Told yer mother, but she never did listen.
Every bit of charge we had. Blow the goddamned ice
apart, I says. We've got to get back. Oh, they sweated.
I'll give 'em that. They laboured till their eyelids was
weighed down wid ice and they couldn't see no more.
I went down meself, boy, lined up on the ropes wid'n.
But what's mortal man when nature sets her face agin
him. Black as hell it wor. And the ice buckling and
rafting beneath us, laughing, I swear. Laughing . . . Hell
isn't fire, boy. It's ice. Black, bitter, cold. Empty.
Filled with the frozen breath of fallen men. Tinkling
over their dead hands like spoons in tea cups. I saw
Jacob in Hell, boy. Out there in the dark.

> *A great gust of wind seems to shake the whole
> structure. He grips Winston.*

She's dragging, boy. Ye're lyin' to me. Lyin'. Like the
glass . . .

WINSTON:
Skipper. We'se got to have this out. We're not at sea.
We're not in a boat. I'm not Jacob. We might be in Hell,
but they's probably better or worse ones. I don't know
yit. Ye're at home, father. Stuck in yer own bed
without the use of yer legs just as ye have been for the
last thirty years and yer daughter and grandsons are
plotting to have ye removed to the Mental. A few more
roars from the bridge and I allows ye'll be gone,
being pushed in a wheelchair down a long corridor
stinking of piss and antiseptic, to yer grave.

> *The old man clutches at him. He shakes him as if
> he were a puppy.*

SKIPPER:
> Ye're a damn fool, boy.

WINSTON:
> Aye, I'm all of that.

SKIPPER:
> A house is a ship. Lights agin the night . . . Some adrift . . .
> Some foundered, some rotting old hulks full of the
> memories of men . . . They's no difference.

WINSTON: *surprised*
> I 'lows that's right enough.

SKIPPER:
> Then I tell ye, boy. This one's adrift.

> > *He sits upright abruptly. He seizes WINSTON's*
> > *shoulder with one hand and points out at the*
> > *audience.*

> Look, b'y. Look. Kin ye see'n.

WINSTON:
> Can't see in front of me own eyelids, Skipper.

SKIPPER:
> Mark me. Look. 'Tis the shape of death, boy. I kin see'n
> jest like that first time, rising out of the drift, moving
> across the ice widout a sound, a man like a cross
> growing up into the sky.

WINSTON:
> Father, they's nothing there. Nothing.

> > *He peers into the SKIPPER's eyes.*

> It don't matter. When all's said and done, ye sees plainer
> than I.

SKIPPER: *relaxing as the vision fades*
> Ah. It's time.

119

He closes his eyes.

SKIPPER:
Ye'll check her moorings, son.

WINSTON:
Aye. I will.

SKIPPER:
That's good, Jacob b'y. That's good.

> *WINSTON draws the blanket about SKIPPER. The storm howls. He goes out softly and stands for a moment on the landing. The light remains on in the SKIPPER's room, but begins to change, narrowing in focus throughout WINSTON's next speech until there is only one white light on the SKIPPER's face giving us the distinct impression that the old man has died. WINSTON looks out of the window.*

WINSTON:
Jesus. They's something out there. Looks to be blowed agin the fence. 'Tis moving.

> *Pause.*

'Tis gone.

> *He rubs his eyes.*

Ach, the old man's got me seeing things now.

> *The storm howls. There is the quality of an inhuman voice in the sound, an intense and savage fury.*

But what if he's right? If we is a ship? Then we's as good as gone. She'll nivir ride this one out. And what's to become of you then, Winston Blackburn? Eh?

> *A door bangs downstairs. WAYNE and MARY are heard. The lights fade up on the kitchen.*

WAYNE: *offstage*
Here, Aunt. Let me help you off with that coat.

MARY: *offstage*
Thank you, Wayne.

> *They stamp the snow off their boots and enter the kitchen, shivering, making straight for the stove. ROSIE is asleep. WINSTON has remained at the top of the stairs. ALONZO is reading yesterday's newspaper in the pantry area.*

I don't remember ever seeing it as bad. Lord bless us, it's a miracle we got home. You were marvellous, Wayne.

WAYNE:
I've driven in storms before, but I'll admit I wouldn't try that again in a hurry. Where d'you think Brad was going.

MARY:
He seemed to be heading for the wharf.

> *ALONZO comes out of the kitchen area.*

ALONZO:
Did ye say ye saw Brad? Mother's worried about him.

MARY:
She might well be. He was running and stumbling like a wild man, talking to himself.

ALONZO:
Didn't ye stop?

WAYNE:
Of course, I stopped. But I'd hardly wound the window down before the ground drift swallowed him up. You can't see a thing out there.

ALONZO:
>I suppose he'll dodge in somewhere. Look at this, Wayne.

>*He takes the newspaper up to him.*

>I've just bin reading the Provincial Report for this area. It's pretty bleak. Unemployment is up. Liquor sales is down . . .

>*WAYNE moves away, averting his face. ALONZO follows him.*

>Fer God's sake, boy. What's wrong with you?

WAYNE:
>To put it bluntly, you stink of fish.

ALONZO: *mildly*
>Oh, do I? I thought the brewis were a bit strong. Must've been some old leggies father put down last year. Never gives 'em enough pickle, father don't.

MARY:
>Wayne, don't forget what I told you. Please.

WAYNE: *slightly irritated*
>Don't worry, Aunt.

>*The radio suddenly crackles and blasts on.*

ANNOUNCER:
>And this reading from Psalm 69. Save me, oh God, for the waters are come in even unto my soul . . . I am come unto deep waters so that the floods run over me . . .

>*The radio breaks down to static and cuts out. MARY makes herself a cup of tea. ROSIE is still dozing in the rocking chair. WINSTON enters and crosses to the table.*

ALONZO:
Amen to that. Now, brother.

WAYNE:
Alonzo. Can't it wait? From the look of things outside, I'm going to be here for days.

ALONZO:
No. It can't wait. Fer me own peace of mind, I'd like to get the business settled once and for all. Where's the tenders.

WAYNE:
I don't have them here. D'you think I'm a fool?

He taps his head.

But I can give you the details.

ALONZO:
I don't trust you, Wayne. I want to see it in black and white.

WINSTON:
Jesus. What have we here, a meeting of great minds . . . Hang on to yer trousers, Wayne. Yer no match fer him.

ALONZO:
Thanks, father. Recognition at last.

MARY:
I've always known what you were, Alonzo. The sins of the parents come home to roost.

WINSTON:
And what sins would they be, Mary. What could Rose an' me have contributed to that.

He points at ALONZO.

MARY:
Moral ignorance . . .

WINSTON: *enraged*
> Moral ignorance. Ye mind yer tongue, woman. Ye can
> call me what you likes, but ye leave Rosie out of this,
> d'ye hear? Ye wouldn't recognize holiness if ye tripped
> in it.

MARY:
> Holiness. I'd prefer to call it childlike simplicity.

> *WINSTON hurls a bottle across the room. The glass
> splinters. The crash wakes ROSIE. WAYNE, who
> is shocked, hurries to MARY.*

ROSIE:
> My . . . What is it now? I were having such a strange
> dream . . . About when we shot Trigger. Do you
> remember, Winston, and had to push him over the
> cliff, on account of he wouldn't fall . . . Winston?

> *He is breathing hard, clutching his chest, and is
> palpably upset as he tries to suppress tears.*

> What is it, love? What's the matter?

WAYNE:
> After all this time, mother. You still don't know? He's
> drunk.

> *WINSTON collapses into a chair.*

ROSIE:
> He's not drunk. And if he was, what business is it of
> yours to be talking to your father so and shaming him?
> It's between him and me, so it is.

> *She bends over him.*

> What is it, love, eh? Has the ould man upset you?

> *WINSTON raises a ravaged face and tries to smile,
> an awful smile.*

124

WINSTON:
Tell ye the truth, love.

He is gasping.

I hardly knows meself.

Suddenly, he grips her hands.

It's me heart . . . It really is. The real one this time.
Ould bugger finally going to demand payment for
services rendered.

He pauses, then faces her, anguished.

What else could I ha' been, Rosie? What else could I ha'
done?

ROSIE: *gently*
Nothing, love. Ye was good enough for me.

WINSTON: *gritting it out*
It weren't good enough, Rosie. Not good enough.
Seems as the times was wrong. Everything changed
afore I knew what to do. The old ones so damned sure
. . . And they . . .

Nodding towards WAYNE and ALONZO.

So certain. Though what about, the Lord knows. And
us, Rosie, us . . . Like rats in a trap, with the Welfare as
bait. I didn't know what to do, so I didn't try. There
didn't seem any p'int. But Jesus, Rosie . . . Jesus . . .

*His inarticulate cry for meaning in life is wrenched
from the gut. It is painful. There is only one
antidote. There has only ever been one.*

ROSIE:
Here, love . . . Here . . . Have a beer . . . It'll calm ye
down.

ALONZO hands ROSIE an open bottle. She puts it in his mouth like a baby. He swigs, then has a clear vision of himself. He takes out the bottle and chokes with laughter.

WINSTON:

Epitaph for a Remittance Man

Stranger, watch when ye're walking on this ground,
Fer Winston Blackburn, he wor drowned,
Not at sea, as ye might suppose,
But in a bottle, held by Rose.

He laughs, then drains the bottle and staggering to his feet, crosses to the rocking chair.

WAYNE:
Mother of God, Alonzo. Did you see that?

ALONZO:
Wayne, I'm impressed. Beneath that tailor's dummy there lurks a heart. You should watch that, brother. It could prove fatal. Now. When do I get that information.

MARY:
Don't have anything to do with him, Wayne. Please.

WAYNE: *crossing to MARY and taking her hands*
It's alright, Aunt. Trust me.

MARY:
It's silly of me, but I have a premonition . . .

WAYNE:
Look . . .

ALONZO:
Come on, Wayne. Stop playing footsie with Aunt Mary and get to the point.

WAYNE hesitates a moment, then crosses back to ALONZO.

126

WAYNE:
  What point?

ALONZO:
  I want duplicate copies of those tenders.

WAYNE:
  You'll get them once I get out of here. Within forty-eight hours.

ALONZO:
  And how can I guarantee that once you've left here with that piece of paper. I was a little hasty there. The dying pains of conscience.

WAYNE:
  You have my word.

ALONZO:
  Oh Jesus! Your word. Come off it, Wayne. You're not talking to the voters now. It's me, remember. We know what we are.

WAYNE: *annoyed*
  What else can I do, man? You're not prepared to accept what I can tell you. I've said you'll get the copies and you'll get them.

ALONZO:
  Alright. I'll have to be content with that, I suppose. But until I get them, I'll take that document back.

WAYNE:
  No.

WINSTON:
  Jesus, Rosie. Turn the radio on, would ye? I preferred 'em fightin' to talking.

ROSIE:
  'Tis on, Winston. The power keeps going or somet'ing.

127

ALONZO:

Look, boy. Give me that paper else I'll blow the whole thing wide open.

He makes a grab for WAYNE's pocket, where the top of an envelope can be seen sticking out. WAYNE jumps back, taking the envelope from his pocket.

WAYNE:

No. I'll tear the damn thing up first.

WINSTON, who has been watching the interchange keenly, suddenly bounds from the chair and snatches the envelope from WAYNE's hand.

MARY:

Wayne.

ALONZO:

Christ. Now we're in fer it.

WINSTON:

Now I'll find out what in the name of God ye were muttering about.

WAYNE goes after WINSTON but he pushes him away, pulls out the document and begins to read.

My God.

He turns to WAYNE.

You bastards. You black, scheming bastards.

WAYNE backs across the room.

Rosie, they've forged me signature. They've written me name to git the Skipper into the Mental. I allus knew they'd like to, but . . .

The words are ground out.

My name! 'Tis all I've got left.

He turns on MARY.

You, you bitch. Ye were in on this.

ROSIE:
Now, Winston . . .

MARY:
Wayne. You should have told me. I didn't want it that way.

WAYNE: *shouting*
It was the only way.

> *WINSTON moves at speed into the parlour.*
> *WAYNE shouts from the door.*

Father. Look. It's for his own good. For the good of everyone in this house. He'd be well cared for, given the best medical . . . My God.

> *WINSTON re-appears carrying a shotgun and savagely shoves WAYNE out of the way as he proceeds towards the bureau, hauls out a draw and produces two shells which he runs into the breech.*

They could keep him alive for years, father. Tell him, 'Lonz.

ALONZO:
Ye keep me out of this. I jest wrote yer name father, that's all. I bin doing that one way or another all me life, ye knows that.

ROSIE:
Winston. Don't.

He turns and raises the gun. Everybody dives for cover. There's a mighty gust of wind and the lights go off as WINSTON fires.

ALONZO:
Christ. Give over, father.

MARY screams and tries to pray.

MARY:
Holy Mother of God, pray for us now and at the hour of our death, amen.

WINSTON curses and fires again.

WAYNE:
You're mad, father.

WINSTON:
Yis. And I suppose ye'd like me to commit meself next. And suppose I goes, I'll go fer something worthwhile.

The lights go up. WINSTON looks about him.

Jesus. Nary one.

He throws the gun down in disgust.

First decent thing I ever wanted to do in me life and the power fails. To hell wid'n.

ROSIE hurriedly retrieves the gun and takes it back to the livingroom. There's a different sound added to the storm, as of a house straining at her shores. The radio blares.

ANNOUNCER:
The Government has resigned. I repeat . . . The Government has resigned . . .

The radio crackles and fades. WAYNE, forgetful of WINSTON, leaps to his feet and rushes to the radio. He beats at it furiously.

WAYNE:
Did ye hear that? For God's sake, come on . . . Come on . . .

WINSTON: *breaking into roaring laughter*
Well, well . . . If that don't beat all.

ROSIE re-emerges and closes the door behind her.

Rosie . . . The government has resigned. That takes care of 'em better than me old shotgun.

WAYNE: *still beating the radio*
Come on.

MARY:
Wayne . . . Don't get so upset. I don't like to see you like this.

WAYNE:
Will you stop nagging me.

WINSTON roars again and claps his hands.

WINSTON:
That's telling ye.

The lights go out again. There's a strange silence, then once again a fearful gust of wind that strains at the very foundations of the house.

WAYNE:
Why in the name of God is everything so dark?

ALONZO:
We're snowed in, b'y. Where the hell are ye going?

WAYNE makes for the door.

WAYNE:
I've got to get to a phone.

ALONZO: *shouting*
Ye won't git ten yards.

In the interior, a clock strikes three.

WINSTON:
'Tis three o'clock. That's the hour, eh, Mary?

ROSIE:
Winston. Kin ye get some candles.

WINSTON:
I couldn't see afore the power went, maid. 'Tis worse
now. 'Lonz. Ye get 'em.

ALONZO:
How the hell do I know where the candles is?

ALONZO fumbles out. ROSIE calls after him.

ROSIE:
An' 'Lonz. Mind ye takes one to yer Grandfather.

WINSTON:
Rosie, me duck. Rosie. Come here. Come here, maid.

*ROSIE finds WINSTON and sits with him on the
day bed.*

Has turned out to be a good day after all, one way or
another. An' I suppose we shouldn't complain too
much, eh? Life's bin as good as it could've bin to the
likes o' we, I suppose.

ROSIE: *softly*
I nivir complained, Winston.

WINSTON:
I knows, maid. And they was times I suppose ye
should've done.

He chuckles.

Does ye mind the time we wor desperate? I wor visiting
your folks and we hadn't had it for a week or more.

ROSIE:
Ye ould Divil.

> *She sighs. A light appears on the landing as ALONZO
> moves upstairs, crosses to SKIPPER's room and
> puts a lighted candle on the chest of drawers. As
> before, a light illuminates the SKIPPER's face.
> What is illuminated now, however, is a Death Mask,
> the actor playing the SKIPPER having left the
> room during the blackout and commotion down-
> stairs. It is essential that the audience is left with
> the illusion that, though the SKIPPER is possibly
> dead, his corpse remains in the bed and it must be
> illuminated in the manner described until the end
> of the play. ALONZO, without checking on the
> old man, comes back down the stairs.*

Ye took me out on the pint, and it cold, the snow hard
on the ground. I nivir t'ought me backside'd ever git
warm agin.

WINSTON:
Ye minds, today I think it wor, when ye said ye cares
fer me.

ROSIE:
Yis.

WINSTON:
Well . . .

He struggles.

I cares for ye to. 'Tis hard to put it into words sometimes. That's all.

ALONZO enters with two candles.

133

ROSIE:
Take one over to yer Aunt, 'Lonz, and bring one 'ere.

He does so. WINSTON gets up, crosses to the
pantry and gets down the remains of the bottle of
moonshine. WAYNE, like a man in a trance, comes
slowly back in.

ALONZO:
Jesus, b'y. What's the matter with you?

WINSTON:
Well. I don't know what's happening, boys. Or what's
happened even. But as we is all here, we might as well
take a little drink together.

He pours a glass and crosses to WAYNE.

Here, boy. Ye lost after all. More than yer dignity, I
allows. Ye've come home. Jine me in a drink?

He proffers the glass.

WAYNE: *blankly*
What? What's that?

WINSTON:
Christ. He's turned to stone. 'Lonz?

ALONZO:
Don't seem to have any choice, do we?

WINSTON:
We nivir did have.

He crosses to MARY, who is sitting numbed and
betrayed at the table. WINSTON puts an arm
around her.

And ye lost too, maid. 'Twas wrong of me to laugh at
yer. I . . . I don't suppose ye'd care to jine me, eh? Fer

all the times we went down the road together to that same school ye teaches at now . . . Hand in hand . . .

To himself.

Up over the hill, the bell ringing, the rivers running over our boots in the first thaw.

He holds out the glass to her. MARY looks at it and reaches for the glass slowly. Then, in a swift movement, she snatches the glass and throws the liquor in his face. He doesn't move. The liquid runs down his face.

They's tears, Mary. I'm crying. Ye've made me cry.

He leans sobbing against the wall. There is an upsurge of wind and storm and the sound of timbers straining, crackling. A distinct sense of catastrophe pervades the atmosphere. The light remains on the SKIPPER.

Into this mixture of fear and pain and expectancy, comes three loud, imperative knocks at the door. Everybody, appalled, looks fearfully in that direction. WINSTON raises his head. He looks aloft and, although not seeing, understands. He whispers . . .

'Tis his token.

He moves slowly to the door.

ROSIE:
Winston!

He opens the door and falls back. The SKIPPER stands there dressed in his Master's uniform, his brass button coat and hat, seaman's boots. ROSIE crosses herself.

Blessed Virgin.

The SKIPPER strides into the room with the vigour of a man in his prime, inspecting the ship.

SKIPPER:
Rosie. Rosie, woman. Git me a glass o' rum.

He pauses in front of WINSTON.

Take the wheel, boy.

WINSTON is confused.

The wheel.

He roars it out, indicating a position downstage. WINSTON stumbles to the spot.

Hold it steady, boy. Steady.

WINSTON reaches, feels for and then grasps the imaginary wheel. We must be in no doubt that for him it exists. He wrestles with it. ROSIE fearfully tenders the SKIPPER his rum. He drains it and gives her back the glass.

Forty years, it's been. Forty years, waiting to see if any o' ye could steer this ship. I give ye fair warning. Have ye anything to say? Good. Comes a time when things has to be brought together as best they kin. When ye has to steer into the starm and face up to what ye are.

He pauses in front of MARY.

Yer mother nivir did that, Mary. Turned her face to the wall and died like an old ewe. But what's lambs fer if they isn't be be sacrificed sometimes.

MARY:
God help us.

SKIPPER:

> North nor East
> And South South West
> From the Round Head Isles
> To Cape Bonavist,
> Steer it clear
> And steer it true
> And the same will take ye
> To Baccalieu

> Did I teach ye that, boy?

WINSTON:

> Aye, Father. Ye did.

SKIPPER:

> Some damn use ye made of it.

> *He crosses to WAYNE and ALONZO.*

> Who are ye?

ALONZO:

> 'Lonz Blackburn, Skipper.

WAYNE:

> Wayne Blackburn, Skipper.

SKIPPER:

> Fust voyage?

WAYNE AND
ALONZO:

> Aye, Skipper.

SKIPPER:

> Ach. That wor always the way of it. But 'tis a pitiful crew for an old haverbeen on his last voyage.

> *He roars.*

> CREW TO STATIONS. Women, git below.

ROSIE and MARY exit, taking the candles with them. WAYNE runs right and grips an imaginary rope. ALONZO leaps upstairs and goes to the edge of the SKIPPER's room, peering out. The sound and the process of disintegration has been building throughout the foregoing.

What's the conditions?

ALONZO: *from aloft*
She's cracking up, Skipper. They's a lead up ahead. Wind East Nor East . . .

SKIPPER:
A lead. Then we'll blast her out. Are ye ready?

ALL:
Aye, Sir. Ready.

SKIPPER:
Listen . . . Listen . . .

Above the storm sounds, very distinctly, comes a seal bark, then another.

Blood and fire and ice. A swile. A swile. I wor right, boys. They've come back. The swiles is back. Newfoundland is alive and well and roaring down the ice pack. A swile. A swile.

There is a moment when all are poised, a tableau, then there is a blackout and the sound of a cosmic disaster, a ripping and rending and smashing, the final release of the insensate fury of nature that has been building throughout the play. There comes a flash that lights up the stage. There is nobody there. Then again, a blackout, the storm dying. The lights go up again, intense, white light that illuminates the threadbare reality of the stage home. Upstairs, the Death Mask is still lit. All fades into the lone quiet crying of a bitter wind.

138

Production Notes

THE SOUND:

It is essential if we are to believe and participate in the tragedy of the Blackburn family, and indirectly, the world that they inhabit, that the storm becomes a living thing, a character whose presence is always felt, if not actually heard, on the stage. Whereas this might make remarkable demands upon sound technicians, it is not so remarkable in reality. The fury of the North Atlantic is well known. Perhaps what is less well known is the elemental fury of that ocean in the early Spring when snow and ice and hurricane combine to create a world in which nothing can live, save the creatures of the sea itself. The history of the early sealing tragedies has been well documented and the conditions that men struggled against, notably in Cassie Brown's epic account of one such disaster in *Death on the Ice* and Farley Mowat's moving testament, matched with David Blackwood's remarkable etchings, The Lost Party Series in *Wake of the Great Sealers*.

I have, however, extended the known reality to encompass the possibility of an environment no longer responsive to the timeless bonding between itself and man which makes communion upon this earth possible, an environment with the will for destruction to match our own and a greater capacity to ensure that destruction, an environment which bred E. J. Pratt's Titanic sinking iceberg, a vast neolithic structure created for just such a time when man's hubris had made him blind to nature, his own matching nature and that harmony which alone makes survival possible.

The storm then has a voice and a presence complementary to the voices and presences on the stage, but one which ultimately outstrips them, engulfs them, destroys them.

THE DIALECT:

I have taken a certain amount of dramatic licence in the presentation of dialect as spoken by the principals.

Rosie, of all the characters, has been untouched by the wider world and her dialect is, as accurately as I am able to determine, authentic.

Winston is a man of considerable experience and education, both of which he seeks to suppress. In consequence, whereas he retains most of the rich verbal inversions which are one of the great strengths of the Newfoundland dialect, I have resisted the temptation to localize his speech, i.e., the substitution of 'd' for 'th' and the dazzling varieties of the use of the aspirant which change from locale to locale about the Coast.

As with both the Skipper and Alonzo, Winston occasionally broadens his dialect under stress or when the sound of the sentence requires it.

Brad, Wayne and Mary have successfully suppressed their native speech and of the three, only Mary, under pressure, sometimes reverts to the older and more satisfying use of the personal pronoun.

GLOSSARY OF TERMS:

conning through the gut	steering through a narrow passage between two points of land
swiles	seals
harp	the harp seal — generally refers to the mother
whitecoat	the baby seal
bousy	grey haired
dogfish	shark
slob ice	ice formed in harbours by frost as distinct from pack ice
gaff	sealer's saviour, now banned. A stout stick, heavily bound, with a two pronged iron hook at the end. It was used to club the seal; for drawing pelts across the ice; for survival when the sealers fell through.
mauzy	hazy
capsize me cock	urinate
barrelman	lookout
scad/dwigh	a light shower of rain or snow
steerings	arctic terns
Divil wettin' his Mother	a few spots of rain when the sun is shining
wharf junk	piece of a large timber used for the base of a wharf
onct	once
chanst	chance
nar, nary	no, none
crackie	mongrel pup
dress me leg	to have intercourse
splits	kindling wood
sculp	skin

The refrain chanted by the Skipper at the close is part of a much longer poem, by which schooner men of the East Coast of Newfoundland committed sailing instructions to memory. The Round Head Islands, Bonavista, and Baccalieu are all critical landmarks on the voyage round the Coast.

TALONBOOKS — PLAYS IN PRINT 1975

Colours in the Dark — James Reaney
The Ecstasy of Rita Joe — George Ryga
Captives of the Faceless Drummer — George Ryga
Crabdance — Beverley Simons
Listen to the Wind — James Reaney
Esker Mike & His Wife, Agiluk — Herschel Hardin
Sunrise on Sarah — George Ryga
Walsh — Sharon Pollock
Apple Butter & Other Plays for Children — James Reaney
The Factory Lab Anthology — Connie Brissenden, ed.
The Trial of Jean-Baptiste M. — Robert Gurik
Battering Ram — David Freeman
Hosanna — Michel Tremblay
Les Belles Soeurs — Michel Tremblay
API 2967 — Robert Gurik
You're Gonna Be Alright Jamie Boy — David Freeman
Bethune — Rod Langley
Preparing — Beverley Simons
Forever Yours, Marie-Lou — Michel Tremblay
En Pièces Détachées — Michel Tremblay
Three Plays by Eric Nicol — Eric Nicol
Lulu Street — Ann Henry
Bonjour la Bonjour — Michel Tremblay
Some Angry Summer Songs — John Herbert
Fifteen Miles of Broken Glass — Tom Hendry
Jacob's Wake — Michael Cook